Mark hadn't held a woman since...

He shoved that thought away, wishing he had the strength to shove away the warm, tender woman pressing into him. Another time, another place, he might have relished embracing Livia Kingston. But right now she could be only a means to an end.

If he lost sight of that, he'd lose the one thing that mattered to him more than his own life—his son.

His hand hit the bare skin at her back, and heat sizzled through his fingertips, tugged at his groin.

Every time he looked at her, he felt some weird connection, not just a male-female lure. This felt as if he knew her on some spiritual level—which made no sense whatsoever.

"Are you okay?" Livia whispered.

Hell, no, he wasn't okay. He lifted his gaze and saw that she felt it, too—a preknowledge of some sort. A shudder rattled through him, clear into his soul.

What the hell was this...this strange sense that Livia Kingston and he were somehow bonded together, sentenced to be with each other for a lifetime...?

Dear Harlequin Intrigue Reader,

Yeah, it's cold outside, but we have just the remedy to heat you up—another fantastic lineup of breathtaking romantic suspense!

Getting things started with even more excitement than usual is Debra Webb with a super spin-off of her popular COLBY AGENCY series. THE SPECIALISTS is a trilogy of ultradaring operatives the likes of which are rarely—if ever—seen. And man, are they sexy! Look for *Undercover Wife* this month and two more thrillers to follow in February and March. Hang on to your seats.

A triple pack of TOP SECRET BABIES also kicks off the New Year. First out: *The Secret She Keeps* by Cassie Miles. Can you imagine how you'd feel if you learned the father of your child was back…as were all the old emotions? This one, by a veteran Harlequin Intrigue author, is surely a keeper. Promotional titles by Mallory Kane and Ann Voss Peterson respectively follow in the months to come.

And since Cupid is once again a blip on the radar screen, we thought we'd highlight some special Valentine picks for the holiday. Harper Allen singes the sheets so to speak with *McQueen's Heat* and Adrianne Lee is *Sentenced To Wed* this month. Next month, Amanda Stevens fans the flames with *Confessions of the Heart*. **WARNING:** You may need sunblock to read these scorchers.

Enjoy!

Sincerely,

Denise O'Sullivan
Associate Senior Editor
Harlequin Intrigue

SENTENCED TO WED
ADRIANNE LEE

HARLEQUIN®

TORONTO • NEW YORK • LONDON
AMSTERDAM • PARIS • SYDNEY • HAMBURG
STOCKHOLM • ATHENS • TOKYO • MILAN • MADRID
PRAGUE • WARSAW • BUDAPEST • AUCKLAND

ISBN 0-373-22696-9

SENTENCED TO WED

ABOUT THE AUTHOR

When asked why she wanted to write romance fiction, Adrianne Lee replied, "I wanted to be Doris Day when I grew up. You know, singing my way through one wonderful romance after another. And I did. I fell in love with and married my high school sweetheart and became the mother of three beautiful daughters. Family and love are very important to me and I hope you enjoy the way I weave them through my stories." Adrianne also states, "I love hearing from my readers and am happy to write back. You can reach me at Adrianne Lee, P.O. Box 3835, Sequim, WA 98382. Please enclose a SASE if you'd like a response."

Books by Adrianne Lee

HARLEQUIN INTRIGUE
296—SOMETHING BORROWED, SOMETHING BLUE
354—MIDNIGHT COWBOY
383—EDEN'S BABY
422—ALIAS: DADDY
438—LITTLE GIRL LOST
479—THE RUNAWAY BRIDE
496—THE BEST-KEPT SECRET
524—THE BRIDE'S SECRET
580—LITTLE BOY LOST
609—UNDERCOVER BABY
627—HIS ONLY DESIRE
678—PRINCE UNDER COVER
696—SENTENCED TO WED

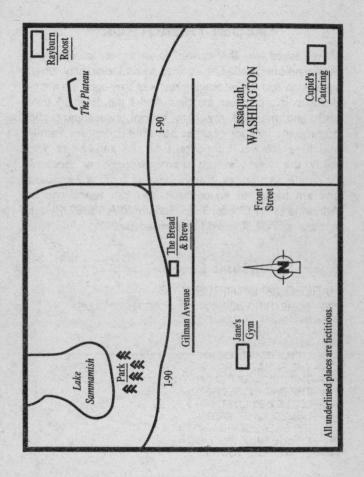

Rayburn Roost

The Plateau

I-90

Issaquah, WASHINGTON

Cupid's Catering

Front Street

The Bread & Brew

Gilman Avenue

Jane's Gym

N

Lake Sammamish

Park

I-90

All underlined places are fictitious.

CAST OF CHARACTERS

Livia Kingston—Thinks she knows what she wants, until she loses it all. Then she's given one month to straighten it out or lose it all for good.

Mark Everett—This sexy caterer holds the key to Livia's survival, but his secrets and undercover identity could get them both killed.

Reese Rayburn—Livia's fiancé is a control freak. What's his is his and no one had better try taking it from him.

Sookie Rayburn—A social icon in her own mind, Reese's mother may not be the ditzy redhead she seems to be.

Jay Rayburn—Reese's uncle once played for the Seattle SuperSonics basketball team, but had to settle for running the company's grocery business, a job that ill afforded him the means to maintain his gambling addiction.

Ali Douglas—Rayburn Grocers' office manager. Is she only eye candy or something much more deadly?

Josh Marshall—Mark's son is the pawn in someone's deadly game.

To Anne Martin and Gayle Webster—
without you two I would never be able to do this which
I love. And always to Larry, who knows why.

SPECIAL THANKS to Priscilla Berthiaume, for her
tender care and handling when the stress was at its
worst, for her creative and constructive input always.

Prologue

The force of the impact against her chest knocked Livia
Kingston off her feet. Pain flashed through her, searing,
sharp, quick, gone in the blink of her eye, replaced by
darkness, solid, unrelenting, enfolding her, embracing
her with the hunger of a new lover. Livia rode with the
sensation that seemed to lift her very being and float
her, weightless and airy like fluff on the wind sailing
upward toward a destination she could not see.

Not darkness. Light. Blinding. Solid. As though she
stood nose to nose with a halogen lamp. But this was
all around her, everywhere she looked. She squinted,
raised a hand to her brow, tried to focus, to pick out
one item, anything she might recognize, a landmark,
something to give her bearing, to tell her where she
was, why she was walking without feeling solid substance, floor or pavement or ground, beneath her feet.
She noticed no noise, or sound, until a sudden dull roar,
like static, stole into the quietude.

She sensed she was not alone, that others, unseen,
walked with her, beside her, ahead of her, behind her.
She felt no confusion or distress issuing from the others, but rather, purpose, relief, expectation and joy. She
alone was confounded, frightened, hesitant. But she

kept moving, gliding along as though on a motorized walkway, unable to stop herself, unable to get off. And still she could see nothing.

Soon the static roar softened, shifted, and she realized what she heard was several voices speaking at once, the murmur of a crowd.

The light began to dim.

Ahead, she made out shapes. Outlines. Gauzy, but recognizable, slowly emerging as if from a fog of light. People. Two men, a woman, a child. Beyond them, the image clearer than the others, stood a tall figure in a hooded robe of pure white silk, the edges trimmed in gold. Behind the robed figure there was a massive, filigree structure that incredibly appeared to be a solid gold gate. Where in the world was this place?

A sense of peace hung in the air, palpable, but it did nothing to ease Livia's distress. She watched as the robed figure spoke to the four people ahead of her, one at a time. He would ask them something, refer to a computer on a golden pedestal to his left, punch the keyboard, then usher the person through the mesmerizing gate.

The closer she came to the robed figure, the more anxious Livia felt. Where was she? She stepped forward. Her turn. As her gaze captured the countenance encased in the pure silk hood, she froze. The face belonged to her deceased grandfather. "P-Poppy?"

She blinked, and the features blurred, then solidified. Not quite her grandfather now. "What's going on? Who are you?"

He touched his cheek. "This is our way to ease the path for new arrivals."

The melodious voice held a trace of her grandfather's Kansas twang.

"New arrivals?" A shiver scurried through Livia. "Where am I?"

"Don't you know?" His glance was a gentle touch. She cringed. "No."

His shaggy eyebrows arched. He eyed her from head to toe as Poppy had often done when inspecting her choice of wardrobe, but this man seemed to suspect something amiss. "What's your name?"

"Name?" That simple detail eluded her for a long moment. She finally managed to blurt, "Livia Kingston."

The robed figure checked the computer, punched the keyboard, then frowned at her. "No. That can't be correct. You're not listed today."

"Not listed for what?"

"For entry."

"Entry into what?"

"Something is very wrong. I need to do a search." He instructed her to place her palm over a lighted pad on the pedestal. Livia's hand complied without her conscious consent. The glowing panel felt warm against her cool skin. The computer began chattering. Data raced across the flat monitor screen, moving too fast for her to read. It stopped suddenly, and the man poked at the screen. "Ah, see, there's the problem. You're not due for sixty more years."

"Sixty years?"

He spun toward her, his robe swishing. "Why do you keep repeating my words?"

"Because I don't know where I am or what's happening to me."

"Happened."

"Happened?"

"See, there you go again."

"Please." She reached for him, then pulled back. "What happened to me? How did I end up here, wherever here is?"

He pressed his lips together, a favorite gesture of her grandfather's. "Why, this is the entrance to Heaven. I'm called the Processor. It's my duty to make certain no one is processed through these gates who isn't in my files. You're not due for sixty years. What are you doing here now?"

Heaven? No. It couldn't be. "I'm dead?"

"It won't do to deny the obvious." He tsked, something else reminiscent of her grandfather. "Just how did you manage to die?"

"Doesn't Heaven keep track of these things?" Livia could hardly take in the news that she'd died, let alone recall how that had come to be.

"That's not my area." He gazed hard at her. "Can't you recollect?"

She closed her eyes on a sigh, straining to think back. "All I remember is something hot hitting me in the chest."

"A bullet, perhaps?"

"A bullet?" She shook her head. "I hardly think—"

"Oh, yes," he interrupted. "That might be it." He consulted the computer again. "Each day, I have a list of new inductees. You are not on that list, but there is someone who was to have died at 2:58 this afternoon from a gunshot wound. A hapless chef. You are definitely not him."

"Well, obviously." Livia couldn't believe her ears. If she'd ever thought of it, she'd assumed Heaven was run with an efficiency that would shame the most organized company in the world. But this person? Saint?

Angel? Whatever. Seemed as clueless as a Valley Girl. "Are you saying that I somehow died in place of this chef?"

"So it appears."

Her hands found her hips. "Don't you guys up here guard against mistakes like that?"

"We 'guys' only have so much influence in these matters. Usually things go as planned, but occasionally, as now, something or other goes awry. This really messes up my record keeping."

"Your record keeping?" Her voice held a wild tone that matched the fear and distress whipping her insides. "Let me tell you, this messes up my life pretty badly, too. I'm getting married tomorrow. Or didn't you know that, either?"

"I did know that, actually. Quite by accident, as it were."

The thought of her wedding, her fiancé, all that she had lost, hit Livia and weakened her knees. "Oh, dear God, I can't be dead."

"Please, Ms. Kingston, don't bring God into this. We try not to bother Him with trivial mistakes."

"Trivial? To you, maybe. But to me..." Oh, this was just awful. Was she being punished because she'd dared raise herself above the life she'd known as a child, because she'd presumed she actually deserved to marry a rich man instead of a pauper? She nearly laughed at the foolish thought. People weren't gunned down for bettering themselves. Besides, she loved Reese. He was perfect for her. In every way. "Oh, God, please, I can't be dead."

"Shh. Don't keep saying that." The Processor glanced around as though expecting a bolt of lightning to strike them. He leaned toward her, his voice lowering to a whisper, his expression odd, conspiratorial. "There might be a way out of this...for both of us...if you're willing to go along."

A way out of this? Her heart leapt, and Livia whispered, "You'll send me back? I can live again?"

"Well...yes." He flicked a glance beyond her. "But actually, it's *relive*."

"I'll do it." She couldn't contain the eagerness spreading through her. "Now. Please. Hurry."

The Processor motioned her closer and lowered his voice again. "It's not that simple. First, you must understand and accept the conditions."

"Oh, sure," Livia said, rolling her eyes. "There *would* be conditions."

The Processor's expression darkened and she feared she'd done something to make him change his mind. She straightened, clutching her hands together, berating herself.

He said, "You'll be going back only to relive this past month, February."

Livia frowned. "I don't understand."

"That's all the time I'm authorized to give you. You have exactly twenty-seven days to change what happened to you. To change your fate. One month to figure out why you died instead of the chef and to make sure it doesn't happen again."

The shortest month of the year. She felt a shiver of apprehension. "What if I can't stop the inevitable. What if it does happen again?"

His eyes were grave. "Then I will have to process you."

She glanced at the huge gleaming gate and swallowed hard over the lump in her throat. She supposed when her time came she would willingly, happily, go through those portals, but now was not that time. She had to make sure she didn't show back up here in twenty-seven days. No matter what she had to do to prevent it. "Okay. I understand."

And she did.

All she had to do was find this loser chef, whoever he was, and see to it that *he* took his own bullet. "Are you going to show me a picture of this chef on your computer, so I'll know him when I meet him?"

The Processor's cyebrows lifted again, this time with incredulity. "I have no such capability on this computer. It is for record keeping only."

"Well, then how will I find him in the short time I'm allotted...?"

"You already know where to find him."

"I most certainly do not."

"Yes, you do. He's the reason I knew you were being married tomorrow. He's catering your wedding."

Chapter One

DREAM? OMELET

Ingredients: 2 Cups Wishful Thinking
1 Cup Denial
Stir well, serve raw

Livia breathed in the scent of cinnamon and coffee and pried open her eyes. Sunshine angled through closed miniblinds that covered the large window and dusted the frilly pink-and-white decor with a hazy pastel light. She saw solid, little-girlish furniture—twin four-poster beds, matching chests of drawers and hope chests. No fluffy white clouds, no filigree gate made of pure gold, no silk-robed Processor. A relieved laugh burst from her. "That was some nightmare."

But that was all it had been. A nightmare. Brought on by prewedding jitters. She had no reason to be frightened. She was perfectly safe here in her parents's house, in the bedroom she'd grown up sharing with her older sister, Bridget. She fingered the headboard where she'd written her name in pink paint. She and Bridget had both done it, each claiming their own space, making their own mark. Her sister's writing, round and sweeping like Bridget herself, the *i* dotted with a heart; Livia's crisp and slanted, without flourish, all business.

These days Bridget ran the Bread and Brew, a popular sandwich and coffee bar, where she made her own breads and pastries. Livia kept the accounts for Jane's Gym and daily conducted two aerobics classes. The perfect job. Getting paid for exercising her brain and her bod.

She lifted her arms high above her head and stretched. She'd given up her apartment two months ago and moved back home to make sure every detail was perfect for the wedding. *Her wedding. Which was today. Yes. Today.* She gave a joyous hoot and shoved off the covers.

She was whole. Alive. Not an angel-wannabe, but human. If not, she wouldn't need to relieve herself so badly. She hurried to the bathroom, took care of business, then stripped and glanced in the mirror, her gaze going to the spot between her small breasts as though she sought telltale signs of...a bullet wound?

She groaned. That darned spooky dream had her rattled more than she was admitting to herself. Silly, of course, but also curious. How had she conjured up such nonsense? Dying from a gunshot meant for someone else? A chef, no less. The man catering her wedding, no less. Heck, she'd never even met Mark Everett. He'd been hired by her fiancé's mother.

She forced her mind from the matter, wishing the nerves in her tummy would settle down. She glanced at her reflection, her gaze scanning the length of her delicate-boned, five-foot-four frame. She pinched the flesh at her waist. If she gained an ounce her gown wouldn't fit. She pulled out the scale and with a shuddery breath stepped on to it. The digital numbers flashed unsteadily then settled on one-fourteen. Exactly right. Livia exhaled a pleased sigh.

Food had once been an issue, one she'd overcome. Now, Livia ate only to sustain life, and hated that she couldn't make her parents and seven siblings see the importance of that. Charlie and Bev Kingston were overweight, they'd given birth to, and raised, eight overweight children, all of whom continued the tradition to this day. All except Livia.

She started the shower, grabbed a towel and facecloth, and stepped beneath the warm water. In grade school, classmates had teased her unrelentingly. She'd felt ashamed. Of herself. Of her whole family. She knew her brothers and sisters were also being tormented. They had to have been. But she couldn't bring herself to ask or to share her own hateful experiences with them.

She remembered well the day it all changed. The day she took control of her life. It had been the week before her eleventh birthday. She'd handed out invitations to the party her mother was throwing for her, then later in the lavatory, she'd overheard two girls she thought were her friends laughing about "Lumpy Livia" eating the whole cake herself. It was the deepest cut. Even now, it pained her to remember.

She had, however, turned that negative into a positive. She'd determined to lose the weight and never gain it back. But she'd gotten no support at home. She'd informed her mother that in future she'd be having only salads and fresh fruit for her meals. Mom had patted her hand condescendingly and told her that was such a nice idea, but with ten mouths to feed, she had no time and no money to make separate meals for everyone. Livia would have to eat what everyone else ate...or go without.

Livia knew girls who "went without," bone-thin wraiths who were starving themselves to death. She wasn't about to lose her health along with the weight, but her mother's suggestion held some merit. She wouldn't go without, but she would eat less. Every day, a little less.

Soon the weight began to go.

To hasten it along, she'd begun running up and down the stairs until her father complained she'd wear down the risers. She'd taken to the concrete steps on the back porch, teaching herself the benefits of aerobics. The weight had come off slowly, but it had come off and every pound shed had encouraged her to lose another. The heady sense of control it gave her was delicious, all she needed to sustain her.

She didn't consider herself a control freak, Livia thought, shampooing. Bridget had accused her of it though. What she was, was fussy. At work, and in her personal life, she wanted everything "just so." It was the only way she could ensure there would be no mistakes, no last-minute disasters. *Like the disaster in her nightmare.* That was why she'd kept her finger on the pulse of every aspect of her wedding arrangements.

Well, all except one.

The one arrangement that seemed to be causing her the most problems now.

She'd wanted her future mother-in-law to feel part of the wedding in some big way and had been delighted when Sookie Rayburn suggested she'd like to handle the one aspect of the wedding Livia had dreaded dealing with: the food. Sookie, the consummate gala thrower, had planned hundreds of fetes and knew exactly what the Rayburn wedding guests would expect.

She had given Sookie free rein to chose anything she liked, including the cake. Livia especially didn't want to select a cake. She reached for the tangerine body scrub and loofa, pushing back the old hurts. She hadn't touched cake since she was eleven. Was dreading that traditional piece being finger-fed her by her groom. Didn't care if it was the lightest white or the darkest chocolate. Cake represented the old Livia. She avoided it like a plague. But she denied herself nothing else, just kept the portions limited. Small.

She stepped from the shower, wrapped a towel around her short streaked-blond hair and dried off with a second towel. She returned to the sink, to the mirror. Instead of her usual morning peakedness, there was a pink blush to her cheeks. Her nerves, no doubt.

The scents of cinnamon and coffee hit her again, the teasing aromas wafting from the kitchen via the heater vent. Her mother had obviously gone all out, making French toast and sausage for her brood, several of whom had arrived yesterday and were crowded into the five other bedrooms on the upper level.

She glanced at the clock. Nearly eight. The ceremony was at two. She had tons to do yet. She went to her closet and pulled out some jeans and a sweatshirt. Later she'd luxuriate in a bubble bath and dally over the other pre-wedding preparations. For now, she wanted to eat, wanted the company of her raucous family whose incessant chatter usually drove her crazy, but today would bolster her confidence, chase off her jitters.

She glanced at the closet door again and felt as though something were missing. It didn't dawn on her until she stepped into her fuzzy slippers. Her wedding gown. For the past four weeks it had hung on that door, a plastic dust cover over it. Her mother must have taken it to press out last-minute wrinkles.

She hurried into the hallway, surprised not to run into at least one of her siblings. All along the corridor the doors were closed. She caught no expected conversation coming from within the rooms. Livia frowned. Were they all already downstairs?

But no chatter rose to greet her as she descended to the kitchen, and Livia wrestled the disquiet tickling her brain as she followed her nose to the source of delicious and tempting smells. She was surprised to find her father alone at the huge table. Had she beat the others down here? She must have.

Charlie Kingston's bald head leaned over the morning newspaper, his half glasses resting on the tip of his nose. His round belly butted the edge of the table as he dug into his coffee and a stack of French toast and sausage.

Her mother, as pudgy as her father, stood at the stove, her favorite place in the kitchen, wearing a stained apron over a green-and-blue polyester pants outfit. Her cap of curly brown hair was laced with gray threads, each earned, she boasted, from one antic or other pulled by her children over the years.

She beamed at Livia, her blue eyes twinkling. "Morning, Livie. It's so wonderful having someone here to cook for besides your father."

"Then you must be in seventh heaven this morning," Livia said, thinking of Ted and Terry, the twins; Chad and Matt, her younger brothers; and Sierra, her oldest sister. All had arrived last night, along with Ted and Chad's girlfriends. Only Bridget lived in town, and she would be here before noon.

Livia helped herself to a cup of coffee. "Do you want me to put out the other mugs?"

"Why, whomever for?" her mother asked, her eyes narrowed in confusion.

Livia frowned, wondering if her ever-sharp mother was losing it, until she glanced at the table and felt a wave of dread. It was set for three. It struck her then that the house was eerily quiet, not from a houseful of sleeping siblings, but because there was no one else there except she and her parents.

Why? Where were they? Her mouth dried at the unthinkable answer that occurred to her. She pulled out a chair and dropped into it, fiercely ignoring the quickened beat of her heart, the uneasy flutter in her belly. "Mom, did you take my gown from my closet door this morning?"

"Your gown?"

"My wedding gown."

"Your wedding gown?"

Lord, she thought, *Mom is repeating what I say—as I did with the Processor in my nightmare.*

Her mother blinked, her chubby face flinching. "The same wedding gown we're shopping for today?"

"Today? No. I bought it weeks ago."

"You did?" Her mother gaped. "Then why are we meeting Bridget at the Bread and Brew in an hour?"

"But I..." Ice washed Livia's veins.

"Do you have a fever, dear?" Bev felt Livia's forehead.

"I'm not sick." Livia pulled back from her mother's look of alarm.

Bev blew out an aggravated breath. "I've been in

and out of your room this past month and I haven't seen hide nor hair of a wedding dress hanging on your closet door.''

"Maybe she stuck it *in* the closet," her father suggested, stuffing another huge bite into his mouth. "What's it look like?"

"Like a wedding dress, of course. White satin..." Livia said on a rush of fear, but she couldn't continue. She squeezed her eyes shut and tried picturing the dress she'd chosen to be wed in. Nothing. Not one single memory of it.

She gripped her coffee mug with both hands to keep them from trembling. Her mouth had gone as dry as the napkins tucked beneath her father's chins. Somehow she found the courage to ask, "What's today's date, Dad?"

He glanced up from his paper. "Are you serious?"

Her mother levered cinnamon-swirled French toast slices onto her plate, eyeing her with fresh concern. "You're starting to scare me, Livie. Please, eat. It will make you feel better."

"I'll have a few more of those, Mama."

"Of course, Daddy-kins." Her mom kissed her dad's forehead and scooped more of the steaming bread onto his plate, killing him with kindness and cholesterol and insuring, if not a heart attack, a severe case of diabetes.

"Dad, the date?"

"Oh, for heaven's sake." Her father groaned, his expression sympathetic. "You've just got a bad case of the pre-nup heebie-jeebies, princess. If you ate more your stomach wouldn't always be in knots. So dig into your mama's grub and all that ails you will be cured."

But Livia had lost her appetite. She took a sip of

coffee, her gaze moving to the banner across the top of the newspaper. The coffee landed in her stomach like a block of ice, and she felt an odd, electric tingling around her neck. *February 1.* No. It couldn't be true. That would mean... No. It had been a dream. A nightmare. She hadn't really died and been given a chance to relive the month of February.

Or had she?

She started to rise, but her legs were boneless and she sank back onto her chair. Her mother took her own place at the table. "Oh, Livie, you're not eating. Your food is getting cold."

Not as cold, Livia would bet, as the blood flowing through her veins. *Not as cold as something touching the flesh between her breasts—in the very spot she'd looked earlier for the bullet wound.* The thought brought her hand to her chest. There was a solid lump beneath her sweatshirt. With a jolt, she realized that whatever the lump was it hung on a chain around her neck.

She hadn't put on any jewelry.

She caught hold of the chain and pulled the object from beneath her shirt, gripping it in her palm, her curled fingers all that kept her from collapsing in a pile of trembling nerves. The object dug into her flesh. She opened her fist, knowing what she would see.

The bullet.

But on her hand lay a small hourglass made of solid gold, filled with something that looked, not like sand, but sparkly dust. Stardust? Her throat tightened. There were twenty-seven teeny demarcations on the bottom glass. The dust moved incredibly slow. But it had started to fill to the halfway mark of the twenty-seven.

"What a lovely necklace, dear," her mother exclaimed. "A wedding gift from Reese?"

"Yes, a wedding gift." Livia felt as though her heart were a stone inside her chest. Here was proof positive that the nightmare hadn't been a dream, but reality. A shudder racked the length of her, sobering her as if she'd single-handedly finished off a whole pot of coffee.

If the hourglass was what it appeared to be, she had less than twenty-seven days. She could not waste another minute in denial. She had to figure out what she was going to do. How she was going to permanently avoid her wedding caterer, when he was catering her wedding.

She stared at the food on her plate, shutting out her parents' chatter, her mind racing for a solution, a direction, a plan. And then she had it. She knew exactly what she would do. It was so simple. An easy fix. Livia heard herself laugh. Her parents looked at her as though expecting her to explain the joke. She grimaced and another nervous laugh escaped. "It's nothing, really. Something someone told me at work yesterday."

She excused herself and hurried to the telephone. Sookie Rayburn gave her the name and number she wanted and minutes later she had dialed. The ringing was interrupted by a husky male voice. "Good morning, Cupid's Catering."

Livia inhaled a bracing breath. "I'd like to speak to Mark Everett, please. This is Livia Kingston."

There was a nerve-racking pause. "Ms. Kingston. This is Mark Everett. It's nice to finally speak to you. I'm looking forward to meeting you. What might I do for you this morning?"

"I am afraid that I'm not going to have the opportunity to meet you anytime soon, Mr. Everett." It was a struggle, but she kept her voice level, barely holding at bay the emotions eating her gut. *She was speaking to a man she knew would be dead in twenty-seven days.* "I'm afraid we won't be needing your services for our wedding. I realize this is short notice, but you'll be compensated for any out-of-pocket money or inconvenience this causes you."

"You're firing me?" He sounded so incredulous it tightened the knot in her chest.

"Well, I wouldn't put it that way. I mean, you needn't take offense. This isn't personal or anything." What it was, was the quickest, easiest solution. If she wanted to avoid being shot at the end of the month, then she had to get *this* wedding caterer out of her life—thereby eliminating all possibility of showing up wherever it was that she'd been when she'd taken a bullet meant for him.

She clutched the hourglass to her heart and felt the tension in her chest break; she could breathe again. "Yes, Mr. Everett, you *are* fired."

"The hell I am."

Chapter Two

CONTRITION TART

Ingredients: Pasty crust top and bottom
Filling: Minced crow
Serves: 1

Like hell you're going to fire me, lady. Nobody fired Mark Everett. Certainly not the fiancée of Reese Rayburn. Mark's gut twisted, and he couldn't seem to push the air from his lungs. He *had* to cater the Kingston/Rayburn wedding. His life depended on it. "You aren't serious."

"Oh, but I am," the woman said coolly.

Mark cautioned himself against the hot string of curse words that sprang to mind. Through clenched teeth, he said, "*Why* are you firing me?"

"I said this isn't personal, Mr. Everett."

"Like hell it's not. I take being fired damned personal. So tell me why."

"I said you'd be well compensat—"

"I don't want to be compensated. I want this job. I have a contract signed by Sookie Rayburn and *you.*"

"Well, yes, but—"

"As you said, Ms. Kingston, this isn't personal. I'm building a reputation, a business. Word of mouth is important in this community." His was a three-person operation at the moment. But his two partners weren't the main source of his concern. "Rumors could destroy me if it gets out I've been fired from the biggest, most publicized wedding of the year."

"No, no, no. This will remain between the two of us."

Huh? Was this woman a complete flake? Mark raked his hand across his trim black hair. What was he saying? Of course, she was a flake. Knowing Reese, this little gold digger had an IQ of sixty and a *Playboy*-model body, all silicone and liposuction. "The two of us? Aren't you forgetting Sookie Rayburn?"

"Well, she will have to be told, of course."

"Of course. Trust me, word will spread like melted butter."

"All the same—"

"All the same, I expect my clients to honor their contracts, especially a contract this large."

"Are you threatening me, Mr. Everett?"

She sounded genuinely afraid and Mark wondered if he'd used his prison voice. Damn. He took a breath, mentally stepping back a notch. "I'm not making a threat, just a promise. Fire me and I'll sue you *and* the Rayburns."

"Sue?" The word seemed to choke from her, as though litigation was a foreign concept.

"You've heard of being sued? My lawyer talks to your lawyer, the newspapers write it up, the judge decides to give me all your money." As if Mark wanted anything more to do with judges or juries. He'd had his fill of that crap. There was only one reason he'd willingly face another judge and it sure wasn't for catering the wedding of a bimbo stupid enough to marry Reese Rayburn.

"No. You can't sue me. Or the Rayburns. They'd be horrified."

"Yes, they would." *And I would probably lose completely any chance of my business taking hold in this community.* Consumers didn't frequent establishments whose proprietors sued their customers. He braced for just such a retort from her, but none came. "Don't wait too long. I have food to order. Or my lawyer to call."

She hung up. The phone banging in his ear.

Mark replaced the receiver, his fist white-knuckled on the handset. What the hell was he going to do now? This stupid Kingston woman could ruin everything. What if she called back and told him to go ahead and sue? God, he couldn't risk that. If she hadn't taken him by surprise, he'd have used better judgment. Held his temper. Too much was at stake for him to allow his emotions to cost him the prize.

He inhaled, plowed both hands through his hair; his belly churned. He needed to calm down, regroup, find this Kingston woman, talk some sense into her, figure out what had made her decide to fire him, then fix the problem.

"A problem, Big E?" Candee, one of his two partners, was eyeing him curiously, his Asian eyes slits in his pockmarked face.

"A minor glitch." Mark clasped his shoulder reassuringly. His confidence started to return, his calm. "But nothing I can't handle."

If he couldn't woo the Kingston bimbo with charm, then he'd ply her with his culinary talents. Mark smiled to himself. "Oh, yeah, I'll seduce her with food."

THE BREAD AND BREW occupied an end space in a busy strip mall in Issaquah, Washington, and did a brisk business, even on rainy northwest mornings like this one. The decor favored shades of pastel rose and earthy greens and conveyed a parlor atmosphere, where customers could relax in settings of grouped high-back chairs, or on twin love seats next to a marble-faced gas fireplace. Other, more traditional tables occupied the space near the picture windows.

The rush hour had abated, but the coffee bar buzzed with conversation as hungry shoppers and those seeking a warm respite from the weather enjoyed Bridget's freshly made goodies, the mélange of aromas rampant in the air. Livia swallowed against the mouth-watering scents.

Not that she felt like eating. Her conversation with Mark Everett had squelched her appetite. She'd thought she'd get rid of him easily, but all she'd done was make a bad and scary situation worse. She couldn't afford a lawsuit, and she sure couldn't allow her future in-laws to be sued. Nor could she tell them the reason she wanted to fire the caterer Sookie had hired.

They'd think she was loony.

She supposed all she could do was avoid him completely and insist that Sookie not bother her with a single detail involving the food until the day of the wedding. She had a sudden disturbing thought. If Mark Everett died the day before the wedding, would there even be any food for the reception? Anyone to prepare it, or to set it up, or to serve it?

The drift of her thoughts sickened Livia. Was she really more concerned about her guests not having Beluga caviar and toast points than she was about a person losing his life? She dabbed rain from her cheeks.

Why had she been assuming his life mattered less than her own? Because he was destined to die from a bullet didn't mean he deserved an early death. What if he were just as innocent as she?

She recalled the harsh resentment in his voice, the twang of danger that told her he was not a man to mess with, and her throat felt as though she were strangling. *You have no idea what that man deserves.* She had to worry about keeping herself alive. He'd have to worry about saving his own skin.

She shook off the thought and waved to Bridget. Her sister was behind the counter, working the espresso machine, her long fingers quick and efficient. Four inches taller than Livia, Bridget had inherited their father's large-boned frame, their mother's dark hair and twinkly blue eyes. Her cheeks were pink from her exertions.

Bridget grinned and gestured for Livia and Beverly to meet her at the table she kept reserved for friends and family. A man was already seated there. A stranger. Livia and Bev hesitated, but Bridget hurried over seconds later with a tray laden with her mother's favorite double mocha, Livia's skim milk latte, two other cups and fresh-baked muffins.

"Right on time. My two favorite guinea pigs," Bridget said, sliding the tray onto the table where the man sat and beckoning her mother and Livia to join him.

"A new recipe, Bridget?" Bev hitched her hip onto the wrought iron-chair and reached for one of the plastic-wrapped muffins, her eyes cutting curiously to the man. "Smells yummy."

Livia wondered if her mother meant the muffin or the man.

Bridget seemed less confused. She said, "Banana and orange marmalade."

The man nodded at her mother in acknowledgment, then turned his golden eyes on Livia. She froze, stunned by something almost electric searing the air between them, something unexpected, and sensual, as though he'd stroked some intimate part of her. She sucked in a sharp breath, and somehow managed to slip onto the ice-cream-parlor chair across from him, hating that her cheeks felt hot, that she couldn't break the lock that held their gazes.

There was nothing classically handsome about his slightly skewed features, his nose obviously broken more than once, his mouth aggressive, the lower lip full, his dark lashed eyes unavoidable, riveting. And yet, *he was attractive*. Damned attractive in a blood-heating sort of way that left Livia feeling in need of a cold shower.

Her disturbing awareness of this man startled her. Reese had never drawn this reaction from her. Never made her skin tingle as this man's gaze did. Never made her feel as though she were missing a pleasure she couldn't even name.

She shook herself. She'd faced worse temptations than him—Godiva chocolates, for one—and managed life fine without them. She took a ragged breath. This was silly. She was a happily engaged woman. So, she found this guy attractive. So what? She wasn't dead…yet. She was still allowed to look and admire and appreciate.

Just not touch.

She peeled her gaze off his face, noticing other details about him, such as the massive stretch of his shoulders, the hard muscles of his chest, barely covered by the smoky-blue polo shirt beneath his tweed sports jacket. His forearm rested on a sheaf of papers related, she supposed, to whatever business he intended to discuss with Bridget.

Bev peeled the plastic wrapping from her muffin and took a big bite, sighing with approval.

Bridget gave Livia an expectant glance, as though it were more important that she try the muffin than be introduced to the stranger at their table. Though her heart wasn't in it, Livia pinched a tiny bit of the frosted, butter-rich muffin and forced herself to taste it.

"This one's a winner," their mother exclaimed.

"Definitely, Bridget." She beamed at her sister, who hadn't quite forgiven her for allowing Sookie to do the food for the wedding. Bridget had had her heart set on making the cake. Livia had nixed the idea immediately, using Sookie as her excuse, but the truth was, if Bridget made the cake, she'd expect Livia's constant input. Bridget had never noticed her aversion to cake, and Livia, fearing she'd become the brunt of family jokes, hadn't volunteered the information.

But Bridget was important to her and Livia didn't want bad blood between them, or hurt feelings. She'd suddenly become too aware of the fragility of life, too sensitive to how quickly it could end in the blink of an eye.

"Are you going to introduce us, Bridget, dear, to this young man?" Bev dabbed at the corners of her mouth with a rose-colored napkin.

"Introduce you? I thought you'd met." Bridget looked from Livia to Bev perplexed.

"We haven't had the pleasure," the man said.

Livia's stomach pinched. She *knew* that voice.

He extended his hand to her. "Mark Everett. Your wedding caterer."

The golden eyes challenged her to deny his claim.

"Wha...what are you doing here?" Livia pulled her hands to her chest, bumping the hourglass, shocked again at its presence, at its reminder of how dangerous was any association with this man. The blood drained from her face. Avoiding Mark Everett could prove more difficult than she'd figured.

"Mr. Everett—" Bridget began, but he interrupted.

"Mark," he corrected warmly. "Please call me Mark."

"M-Mark has made me the most generous offer," Bridget gushed, giving him a beaming smile. "He wants me to help make your wedding cake. Isn't that wonderful?"

No! A scream pinged through Livia's mind. This was her second worse nightmare. She gulped a mouthful of latte, then lowered the cup to the table before she felt the foam on her upper lip. She tongued it off, but caught those golden eyes watching, lighting with something earthy and sensuous. She grabbed her napkin.

"Aren't you pleased, Livie?" Bridget's blue eyes flickered with uncertainty, her excitement falling flat.

Livia reached a hand to pat her sister. "Of course, I'm delighted. It's very generous of you, Mr. Everett."

She gave him such a hard smile her cheeks ached. She wanted to strangle him, end his life here and now. He was not only a danger to her, but to her whole family. She stood up. "We are going to be late."

"I'll tell Alicia I'm leaving and to set out some of the new muffins since they've passed the guinea pig test."

Mark Everett caught Livia's arm at the wrist, his

tapered fingers like a human handcuff. "Could you spare me a minute, Ms. Kingston?"

"Sure." Bridget answered for Livia as she stripped off the pristine forest-green apron that served as her uniform. "Mom, could you get my purse and my coat from the office?"

Her mother and sister hurried off, leaving Livia alone with the wedding caterer. She wrenched free of his disturbing grasp and glared at him. "What kind of stunt are you pulling? I told you, you're fired."

He leaned close to her and she caught a whiff of something sweet...vanilla? She'd never known a man who smelled of vanilla.

He put his hands out in a gesture of cease-fire. "And I made threats of suing...but we left the issue unresolved."

Her stomach jumped. She didn't want to be sued, didn't want the Rayburns to be embarrassed, but what else could she do? She couldn't speak.

He kept his voice low. "On reflection, I realized you're probably dealing with a lot of stress. So am I. So, I decided I should come and speak to you in person, ask you what it was that precipitated your wanting to fire me. Whatever it is, I apologize. Let's fix it. I'm sure we can find a solution that works for us both."

"There is no solution."

His frown was just short of a scowl, and she saw again that her first impression of him had been right. He was a man who knew violence. But was he violent? He closed his eyes, seemed to gather his composure, then showed her the warmth of his intense gaze. "Why is the problem without solution?"

Because I don't want to take another bullet meant for you. As though to remind her, the hourglass poked her chest. She gulped more latte. Even if she warned him, told him what she knew, he wouldn't believe her. And it would only make him more determined than ever to sue her and her fiancé. "I just want you out of my life."

"Why? What have I done to incur such vehemence?"

"Nothing." She shook herself. "I told you it wasn't personal."

"Then why do it?"

She couldn't find words to make him understand. With relief, she saw that her mother and sister were ready to leave. "I have an appointment. Goodbye, Mr. Everett."

BUT MARK EVERETT wasn't so easy to be rid of. Livia was trying on a fourth wedding gown at the bridal boutique in downtown Bellevue, viewing her reflection in the three-way mirror of the salon waiting area, when she saw him. Somewhere behind her. Leaning against a clothes rack.

Her heart gave an disquieted leap.

His gaze swept the length of her, assessing. He shook his head in disapproval.

She'd reached the same conclusion. The gown was Bridget's choice, all lacy ruffles and frills. She'd only tried it on to indulge her. God, why couldn't she recall the dress she'd chosen before she'd been shot, so she wouldn't have to waste time doing this again? At the rate they were going the whole day would be gone. But she wanted her wedding to be perfect, and the dress she chose was important. She wouldn't pick something in haste and end up hating it four weeks from now.

"It's gorgeous, dear," her mother said.

Bridget shook her head. "Livie doesn't like it, Mom. Look at the way she's scowling. It was just a suggestion, sis. Try that slinky satin, off-the-shoulder one next. It's kind of pretty in a plain-Jane sort of way."

"Bridget, why don't you and Mom look at the veils and see what you think might compliment a plain-Jane wedding gown? Remember, nothing frilly."

As soon as they walked away, she lifted the hem of her dress, feeling like Scarlett O'Hara on a rampage, and stalked to where Mark Everett stood. "Why are you following me?"

He leaned closer and she caught that hint of vanilla mixed this time with damp tweed. "Please."

There were rain specks on his cheeks and something soft in those hard eyes that she hadn't seen before. It caressed her compassionate nature, made her more aware than ever that if she won this race against time, he would lose.

She banked her anger and gentled her voice. "Please, what?"

"Let me prove to you that I am the best caterer you could have hired."

"And," she said, picking at strands of her cropped hair. "If I'm unwilling...?"

The softness disappeared from his eyes, replaced by determination. "Then I'll have to keep trying to change your mind."

"I see." She had a feeling he'd follow her from bridal shop to bridal shop if she refused him. She scrubbed her temples with her fingertips, then sighed and rescued the hourglass from the lacy folds at her chest. It felt hot against her palm. A talisman. That tied the two of them in an uneasy union. There was no avoiding it. Fight as she may against it, their fates were intertwined. "Just how do you intend to prove your case?"

He ran a hand over his short hair. "Let me cook for you."

"You're asking me to be *your* guinea pig?"

"If you want to put it that way. I'd like a personal recommendation from you after the wedding. In order to give that, you'll need to approve each dish for the reception."

Lord, food. She closed her eyes. The one thing she'd struggled so hard to overcome. Her heart beat harder. Why had she thought she could earn the right to live without walking through fire? That it would be easy—instead of as painful as birth?

"Ms. Kingston?"

She inhaled shakily. What was that old saying—keep your friends close, your enemies closer? Maybe she needed to take a different tact on this. Perhaps the only way to avoid being shot in less than twenty-seven days was to get to know this man. To find out what he was hiding.

Why someone was going to kill him.

She swallowed over the lump in her throat. Her way, she would be in control. Could manage her destiny. "Okay, Mr. Everett. I'll give you a second chance."

Like the one she'd been given. But his second chance was a chance to die. She flushed.

"I believe in second chances," he said, as though she'd just done him a huge favor.

She doubted he'd feel that way at the end of the month, when he stood before the Processor. No. She couldn't afford to feel sorry for him. Couldn't allow that to derail her. "I'll take over the handling of the food for the wedding on one condition. If, at the end of one week, I still want to fire you, you'll go without an argument.''

"Two weeks."

He looked so desperate, so contrite, she ignored her better judgment. Why did she feel as though she were making a deal with the devil himself? She grimaced. "Only if you promise not to sue."

He smiled, a sexy lopsided tilt of his intriguing mouth, the warmth going all the way to his eyes for the first time. A disquieting heat stroked through her veins. He extended his hand. "Deal."

She drew in a shuddery breath, nodded and accepted the handshake. "Deal."

His flesh was warm, dry, reassuring, but Livia was not reassured. She felt as though they'd just sealed their fates and that in the end, they would both be sorry.

Chapter Three

PEANUT BUTTER AND JAMMED

Ingredients: Big and Little Boys
Stir in Patience and Understanding
Serve: Hot and Cold

The next day, Livia spied her future mother-in-law's red Jaguar sitting out front of the offices of Rayburn Grocers Inc. in Issaquah and pulled into the lot beside it. She glanced at the concrete building. Long and wide, with several loading docks, the warehouse quartered the tons of food supplies the company distributed to local restaurants.

Reese's grandfather had started the business in the sixties, passed it on to his two sons Jayson and Phillip on retirement, and now, since Phillip's death over a year ago, Reese and his uncle Jay shared the helm. The company was not the largest food distributor in the Seattle area, but it held its own.

Food. It was the bane of Livia's existence, tempting her at every turn. *As long as I control it, it can't control me.*

She clenched her jaw to keep from grinding her teeth

as her mind shifted to the deal she'd made with that devil of a caterer. Thanks to him, she still had no wedding gown. He'd rattled her so badly, she hadn't been able to concentrate. She'd thought after she'd agreed to give him a two-week trial that he'd leave the bridal gown shop, but she'd been wrong. As she'd assessed her reflection in the mirror—her mother and Bridget giving nods of approval to the slinky satin, off-the-shoulder, plain-Jane dress—Livia had glimpsed Mark Everett's hot golden gaze staring back at her, like twin fires of hell stroking her, making her feel downright sinful in the virgin-white satin and lace, as though it were the skimpiest, most man-luring scrap of red-hot lingerie.

She couldn't get it off fast enough. Damn that man. Why did he have such an odd effect on her? Was it because she knew he was marked for murder? And he didn't know? Or was it something else? No. She didn't want to examine *that.* With the exception of one little glitch, her life course was mapped out.

She made herself get out of the car and go inside. The front office looked much like any other: durable linoleum on the floor, receptionist's desk center stage, waiting chairs hugging the windows, posters of Rayburn's top-selling food packs on the walls, and Ali Douglas, a pretty, buxom brunette with a quick smile to greet visitors. She forced a smile of her own. "Hi, Ali. Is Mrs. Rayburn here?"

"She's with her son."

"I'll wait then." Livia took the Naugahyde seat closest to the door. She'd decided the best way to free up her time was to delegate to others as many of her wedding planning tasks and responsibilities as possible, but she wasn't looking forward to explaining to Sookie

Rayburn why she, Livia, would now be selecting the food.

Including the cake.

She'd thought of little else all day, the old fear holding her by the throat, scolding her for every bite she'd put into her mouth. What if she chose a dress now, then gained weight over the next two weeks and couldn't fit into it or had to have the seams—horror of horrors—let out before she wore it? The very idea had her taking on an extra aerobics class this morning—as though burning calories before consuming them would keep off fat. She'd lost all logic.

She felt sick.

"You really shouldn't wear that particular shade of green, dear. It makes you look rather...ill." If not for the clamor of Livia's thoughts, Sookie Rayburn could not have sneaked up on her. The woman weighed all of ninety-eight pounds dripping wet, but walked surprisingly heavy on heels that struck the floor with the resounding clip-clop of a shod horse. "Reese is on the phone, but he should be off soon."

"Actually, I wanted to talk to *you*—if you can spare me a few minutes."

Sookie's tomato-red hair swept off high cheekbones and her skin stretched to wrinkle-free smoothness. At Livia's request, her taut eyebrows gave a slight arch, which Livia suspected was all she could lift them. She stood and Sookie glanced toward the receptionist, whom she'd often said thrived on gossip about the Rayburns. Ali appeared to be working at something on her computer, but even Livia suspected she hung on every word.

Sookie said, "Let's use the conference room. Ali, could you bring us each a black coffee?"

Once they were settled at the table, steaming cups of the hazelnut-scented mud Ali called coffee in front of them, Livia asked, "How did you come to engage Mark Everett to cater our wedding?"

"Bitsy recommended him."

Bitsy Wallingford. Sookie's best friend since college and hostess extraordinaire. Livia shoved one hand through her short streaked-blond hair and moved the coffee aside with the other. "I see."

Curiosity pooled in Sookie's austere gray eyes. This was the second time Livia had spoken to her about the caterer. "Is there a problem with him, dear?"

If you only knew. She shook her head. "No. I was just wondering."

"Well, then, let me tell you something. Bitsy says—" She broke off, scooting closer, eyeing her in a conspiratorial way, as though they were girlfriends sharing a naughty secret. "—his *pastries* are positively wicked."

Sookie made it sound as if "his pastries" were part of his anatomy. The image of that incredibly sexy man blinked through Livia's head, and her cheeks heated. How positively wicked anything about Mark Everett might or might not be was not something she wanted to imagine, or to discuss—especially with *this* woman. She took a deep breath and got to the point of her visit. "I have a huge favor to ask you."

Sookie lifted the disposable cup to her collagen-enhanced lips, the white plastic a stark contrast to her wine lipstick. "Okay."

"I've decided to consult with Mr. Everett myself about the food."

"Oh?" She looked crestfallen, as though she were

being robbed of her only chance to sample the wicked pastries. "I—I thought—"

"My sister Bridget is involved now," Livia rushed to explain, exploiting the animosity Sookie and Bridget shared. "And I thought maybe since you and she don't see eye to eye on things…that I could count on you to handle all of the flowers instead."

"The flowers?" Delight brought a smile. Sookie arranged flowers as if she'd not only excelled but majored in it in college. If the Rayburns ever went broke she could open a florist shop and recoup the family funds in no time. Sookie clawed the air with her designer acrylic fingertips. "Now that's something I could dig my nails into. Have you decided on what colors you're using yet?"

She hadn't even picked the colors for her wedding. Livia bit back a groan. At this rate, even if she survived to marry Reese in twenty-six days, she was in real danger of having none of the wedding planned. What she couldn't understand was why she, who was the most anal female she knew, hadn't nailed down every detail months ago. It wasn't like her to put anything off, but she'd been putting all of this off. Until this moment, she hadn't thought to question her bizarre behavior.

"Colors?" Sookie prodded.

Livia glanced wildly around, but her mind's eye saw only gray as though she'd lost the ability to detect other colors. "Er, I'm not sure."

Sookie said, "Well, as the wedding is taking place shortly after Valentine's day and right before the Ides of March, it's a great time for roses and carnations. I'd suggest red, shades from the palest pink to the hottest crimson. Yes, yes. Red."

A small spot of red appeared in the center of the

gray filling Livia's mind, spurting like blood from a gunshot wound. The gruesome image snapped her out of the weird mental fog, reminding her just how little time remained. She caught the tiny hourglass between her forefinger and thumb, and as if it were a magic camera, she saw the bridesmaid dress Bridget had tried on yesterday, a satiny teal that had actually looked drop-dead gorgeous on her. *Of course. Teal. Rich without being gaudy.* She said, "I've decided on teal and silver. So, maybe white flowers would be best."

Sookie puckered as though her coffee were bitter lemon juice. "White is just so…unimaginative."

"In your hands, Mother, it will be inspired." Reese Rayburn strode into the room with the agile bounce of a dedicated jogger. He wore a silk shirt, tie and slacks in a monochromatic charcoal, beneath a tan sports jacket. Livia had met him last year at Jane's Gym, the unisex fitness center where she worked. He had dark red hair, storm-blue eyes, and an intensity like bottled energy. He pecked her on the cheek. Most of his kisses, she realized, were pecks. "Darling, I'm glad you're here. Do you think you could pick up Joshie this afternoon and take him to the park? I promised, but now I've got a meeting I can't get out of."

"Ah, sure." The hourglass heated between her breasts, reminding her that she didn't have time for trips to the park with children, but she would take the time. Josh was Reese's nephew, the son of his deceased half sister. Sookie's stepdaughter. Livia and Reese were going to adopt him right after the wedding and raise him as their own. She adored the little boy. Besides, she had just crossed two items off her list of wedding planning tasks. Flowers and colors. She could spare a few hours for Josh.

"I won't be able to meet you for dinner tonight, either," Reese said. "New clients. From out of state. They're opening a chain of restaurants in the area and Jay and I are winin' and dinin' 'em. Could be a big coup if we land this account. Thing is, I'm not sure how late I'll be."

"That's okay, I couldn't—"

"You ready, Reese?" Jayson Rayburn, Jay-Ray to his friends, slapped the door frame. Though he was Reese's father's brother, he was closer to Reese's age.

"Right with you, Jay."

"Don't know why we're in such a hurry. Airport security being what it is, ten to one we'll be standing around waiting an hour before they hit baggage claim."

Reese laughed, planted another peck on Livia's cheek, then hurried after his uncle, brushing her off like so much lint from his spotless coat, not even hearing that she'd been going to break their dinner date. That she had plans...with another man, *a gorgeous devil of a man...who made wicked pastries.*

Sighing, she said goodbye to Sookie and followed the men out just in time to see Reese gaze at Ali, the receptionist, as though she were a cupcake whose frosting he wanted to lick. Considering the kiss he'd just given her, it would likely be only a flick of his tongue. She smiled to herself at the thought, not even jealous. He was just looking. As she'd looked at Mark Everett. It proved nothing. Reese was human. Male. He was engaged, he wasn't dead.

Both of them "looking" was natural, normal, healthy male/female behavior.

It showed they were...observant, she decided, noting that Reese wasn't nearly as tall as Mark Everett, or as his uncle.

Her mind shifted to Jay-Ray. Just out of college, he'd been drafted by the Seattle Supersonics professional basketball team, but hadn't made the final cut. With his hopes of a sports career dashed, he'd stopped resisting his father's entreaties and joined the family business. He'd used his athletic contacts to increase sales and kept up with his interest in sports, especially basketball.

Reese seemed in awe of him and, though she didn't think that was necessarily a bad thing, she wished he wouldn't blow off Josh whenever Jay snapped his fingers. She didn't doubt this meeting was as important as he said, but Reese was forever promising the little boy this or that, then something would come up—usually with Jay—and his promise and the child were forgotten.

She would have to talk to him about this…after their honeymoon.

She scrambled into her car and headed toward Josh's school. Luckily she still wore her workout clothes and had a soccer ball in the trunk. She stopped at a deli on the way and bought a sandwich, apple and milk for the little boy, knowing he'd be ravenous when she arrived. At the counter, she added a giant cookie to her purchases, to salve his disappointment.

She didn't want him growing up substituting food for love, but sometimes a kid just needed to have a treat. As much as she might complain about her loud, noisy, nosy family, she wouldn't trade them for anything. Didn't even want to imagine how awful it would be to lose a parent, let alone both of them. Poor little guy. Some days she wanted to just hold on to him forever.

THE AFTERNOON was cool with just a hint of dampness in the air, and they had this section of the park near Lake Samammish almost to themselves. Six-year-old Josh Rayburn Marshall had sandy-brown hair, hazel eyes, a spray of freckles across his nose and ears that stuck out just a bit. He was a miniature of his mother, Wendy. Two years ago, Wendy had been fatally shot by her husband, Ethan, who was later found guilty of first degree murder and sent to the state penitentiary where he was currently serving a life sentence with no chance of parole.

Reese claimed Josh didn't know much about it, but Livia knew children heard more than adults gave them credit for. Whether or not he had overheard the adults discussing his parents, she was certain that the one thing the kid did know was that his mommy and daddy were never coming back.

Her heart ached for him.

She rolled the soccer ball to Josh, and he sped forward and caught it between his feet. She beamed at him. "Hey, you're getting pretty good at trapping that ball, mister."

"I been prasticing in the backyard, hitting it off the garage wall."

At his pronunciation of "practicing," she bit back a smile, wincing at the pity that squeezed her throat. He spent way too much time alone. She'd spent *her* childhood wishing she were an only child. She saw now that if God had granted that wish, she'd have been as lonely as this little boy. *When I'm your full-time mom, Josh,* she vowed silently, *I'll do everything within my power to make sure you never feel lonely again.*

She stole the ball from him, then he stole it back, racing away from her toward the two rocks they'd set up as the goal posts. She chased him, and his laugh resounded into the cool air, bouncing off the trees, lighting his eyes, filling her heart.

"Goal!" He kicked the ball between the stones. "I win!"

"Yes, you do." Laughing, her breath puffing, she caught him, hugging him. As his little arms clutched her, hanging on almost desperately, a lump rose in her throat, and her mind snapped back to thoughts of murder, to thoughts of her own death. To thoughts of Mark Everett. Of someone wanting him dead. She still had no idea why. What had he done to make him the target of a murderer? Until she knew that, she could not even guess *who* was after him.

Who *she* needed to avoid at all costs.

A movement behind a tree snagged her attention, grabbed her breath in her throat. A man. In shadow. At the backside of the tree now. As though he'd been hiding. Was hiding. Had been watching them. Was watching them. Waiting to pounce.

Her pulse kicked faster. This area was not that far from where Ted Bundy had once hunted victims. She kept her eyes riveted to the spot where she'd seen the man.

Her hands tightened on Josh, not so firm as to scare him, but solid enough so he wouldn't decide to break lose and chase after the ball, which had rolled down a short incline. "Josh, it's getting late. We have to go. Now. I'm gonna race you to the car. On three, okay?"

"Okay." He seemed delighted with this new game.

"One, two, three." She clutched his hand tight and ran with him across the grass, over bumpy ground, leaping potholes, puddles. Josh squealed with delight.

She hit the tarmac and they picked up speed. They were three feet from the car when he pulled to a stop.

"The ball." He wrenched against her hold. "We forgot it. I'll get it."

"No." She clamped her hand on his, and pain registered in his hazel eyes. His plump cheeks were red from exertion, his freckles more distinct than usual. "I'll get you another ball."

She clicked the car remote, unlocking the doors, yanked open the back door and hurried him inside. "Put your seat belt on. Quick."

"Why?" There were tears in his voice, and she hated that she was scaring him. She locked his door, slammed it shut. She wrenched open her own door. She dove onto the seat, jammed her key into the ignition and grabbed for her door.

But she was too slow.

The man was there. He grasped the door above the window, stopping her attempt to slam it. Her gaze riveted on his strong fingers that were scarred as though a knife or something equally sharp had been dragged across the flesh three times.

He said, "You forgot something."

"Livia! Livia!" Josh shouted. "Is the man going to hurt us?"

Chapter Four

DEVIL'S FOOD

Ingredients: Beefcake and Temptation
Serve: One Bite at a Time

"I'm not going to hurt either of you, Josh." Mark Everett's fiery golden eyes softened to honey as he gazed at the boy. "I'm sorry I scared you. I just wanted to return this."

Livia glared at Mark Everett as he released the door and held the soccer ball out to her. Fury and fear twisted her insides like twin rods of molten steel, hot and sickening. Her chest heaved, and her breath steamed as she stomped to the pavement. "I ought to smack you for scaring that little boy like that," she ground out only loud enough for him to hear. "What the hell are you doing here?"

He raised the black-and-white ball in his battered hands like a shield. "Walking."

"In the same park Josh and I happened to be in?"

"That was a coincidence, Ms. Kingston." His gaze felt like a caress on her cheeks, oddly cooling her anger, calming her worst fears.

But she wasn't ready to let him off the hook. She narrowed her eyes at him. "Yeah, sure."

"I swear." He propped the ball on one hip, then shoved his disheveled black hair back from his brutally handsome face, a face that was all hard planes and deep valleys, the map of a man who'd been treated poorly by life and come out more intriguing despite everything. His expression went earnest, his voice soft. "I meant no harm."

"Then why were you lurking behind that tree like…like some pervert or serial killer?"

"When I came across you and…the boy, I figured—after yesterday—that you'd think I was stalking you or something." His every word was scented vanilla. "But then you ran off and I realized I'd scared you, and I hadn't meant to do that."

She closed her eyes, inhaling sharply. Why did he smell so damned…delicious? Did he drink vanilla? Splash it on his cheeks after shaving?

"I swear, I was just walking."

The hourglass at her chest tingled, and she knew he was lying. Maybe he *had* been spying on her…again. But more likely—considering someone wanted to kill him—he was using this innocent park for some nefarious deed. Perhaps a drug deal. She blanched. Lord, was he a drug dealer? A drug user? She didn't want Josh exposed to anything like that. "You might want to work on your people skills."

Mark winced as though she'd struck a nerve. "Next time I'll make my presence known earlier."

Next time? There wasn't going to be any "next time." No way. "Thank you for returning the ball." She took it from him, their fingertips colliding, the contact sending tiny zaps of current into her flesh. She blinked in shock. What was it about this man that confused her nerves, addled her brains, teased her senses?

He glanced at Josh. "Will he be okay?"

"I'll see to it that he is." She clutched the ball to her thundering chest.

He pulled his gaze from the boy, and there was something in his eyes that hadn't been there before, something deeply tender and sad. He searched her face as though trying to discern whether or not she meant what she'd just said. He cleared his throat. "You'll be there tonight?"

She took a bracing breath and nodded. "At seven."

As he strode toward a car at the other end of the parking lot, Livia climbed into the back seat of her compact and hugged Josh, then handed him the ball and smoothed his mussed hair. The color had returned to his cheeks and he seemed much calmer than she. "I didn't mean to scare you, Josh. I didn't get a good look at Mr. Everett and thought he was a stranger."

"I know 'bout strangers. Mommy teached me. And we learned in school, too." He was gazing out the window toward Mark Everett. "I wasn't scared."

The instinct of children, she thought, comprehending with sudden wisdom that she hadn't felt any real fear of Mark Everett, either, not after that initial burst. Anger. Fury. But not fear... Why was that?

She lifted her gaze and stared at Mark's retreating back, as Josh was doing. The little boy said, "Who is that man, Livia?"

"That's a very good question, Josh." Before she showed up at Cupid's Catering tonight, she was going to go on the Internet to find out whatever it was that Mr. Mark Everett was hiding.

BUT HER SEARCH proved a big disappointment.

Livia had thought you could trace anyone on the Internet. Wasn't that what everyone claimed? That it was "Big Brother" watching us all, recording our lives, our credit histories, our scholastic achievements, our sock sizes. But not Mark Everett's. She'd found his current address, a web page for Cupid's Catering, and that was it. If he'd existed before he'd opened his catering service, as Sookie claimed, four months ago, she hadn't been able to prove it cruisin' the information highway.

On the other hand, her computer skills could fill the hourglass hanging between her breasts. Oh, she could operate e-mail and use word processing and maneuver the Internet enough to do basic searches, even order merchandise. But maybe there was some trick to digging up the kind of information she sought. *Chad.* She snapped her fingers. The youngest Kingston sibling was also the family computer guru. If anyone could help, he could. She sent him an e-mail outlining what she wanted and asking how to go about searching for it.

He hadn't gotten back to her by the time she headed out for her appointment with the caterer, and Livia felt more frustrated than she'd thought possible. Two days had passed—soon it would be three—and she still had no idea who was after Mark Everett or why. She considered point blank asking him, but how could she tell him he was going to die in twenty-six days? Almost twenty-five? And even if she found the courage to tell him, was he likely to believe her? Or likely to think she should be avoided and insist on dealing with Sookie or Bridget to fulfill the contract?

No. She had to get closer to him. Had to figure out

why someone would want to shoot him. It was her only chance to prevent her own death. *And,* once she knew why and who, she *would* warn him. He might still decide not to believe her, she knew, but at least then his fate would no longer be in her hands.

Her head was starting to ache by the time she reached the residential area of old town Issaquah that had been rezoned in recent years for business usage. On either side of this street, pre-World War II homes nestled between elderly trees. Cupid's Catering occupied a corner lot at the end of the third block. The brilliant porch light showed that the house had been painted a tasteful cream with dark teal trim, the exact shade of teal she'd decided on for her wedding.

Talk about coincidences.

She parked in front of the three-story structure and climbed the eight steps to the wide covered porch. A bristled Welcome mat with Cupid's Catering sprayed in teal letters graced the spot beneath the teal door, and a sign beside the doorbell told prospective customers that this business took Appointments Only. The night had turned chilly. She hugged the collar of her coat close to her neck, gathered a steadying breath and knocked.

Mark answered the door. His strong thighs were poured into faded jeans, his muscled arms darkly tanned against a tight white T-shirt, and his whip-thin waist lashed by a teal apron. She'd bet his body fat wasn't over four percent.

Mark studied her face. "Is the boy all right?"

"Not even going to say hello first?" Though she said this in a flippant way, his concern for Josh touched her, stripping away any lingering ire she held toward him for scaring them this afternoon. "He's fine. Really."

Looking relieved, Mark moved aside and she stepped into the foyer. The floor was oak planking, the room wide enough to hold an antique hall tree with mirror and coat hooks, a parson's table spread with business cards, brochures, guest book, and a teal screen that separated this area from the next room. Yesterday, she had never given the color teal a second thought, now it seemed to be everywhere she looked. It was starting to spook her.

She took a sharp breath, inhaling a fragrant fog of delicious odors that made her mouth water, her empty stomach rumble. She hadn't eaten in anticipation of tonight's tasting marathon. She hugged a tablet she'd brought for note-taking, felt a bit light-headed, and increased her grip on the pad as if it were going to keep her on her feet.

"May I take your coat?" he asked.

"Uh, yes." She unzipped the jacket, her back to him as he helped lift it from her shoulders. His breath whispered against her ear, bringing a hint of vanilla into air already rife with ambrosial aromas. Her mouth watered, and she spun to face him. She wore gray wool slacks and a baby-pink angora sweater that she'd spent way too long choosing for a visit to a caterer. His hot golden eyes glowed with approval, and she tugged at the hem of the sweater that barely covered her navel, resisting the impulse to touch her hair.

Of course she was nervous. Not because *he* made her nervous, or even self-conscious, but because she planned to do some covert snooping tonight, if the opportunity arose. The one thing she *had* learned on her Internet search was that his business address was also his home address. He lived in this wonderful old house with too many touches of teal.

"It's warmer in here." Mark ducked around the screen. "I've got a fire going."

She followed, her nerves starting to loosen her tongue. "Bridget was going to come with me tonight. Talk to you about the cake. But she called at the last minute to beg off. The coffeemaker at the Bread and Brew is on the fritz and if she doesn't get it fixed tonight she'll lose a whole morning's worth of business tomorrow." She'd tried enlisting her mom as a last-minute replacement, but she was at bingo. And so, against her best attempts to prevent it, Fate had brought her here to face this man alone.

Perhaps that was better.

Being alone with Mark Everett would give her the chance to observe him, to notice that which she might not have if her sister or mother had come with her. He was a contradiction in many ways. Rugged, dangerous in appearance, yet sweet-smelling and clean, concerned about a child as many men might not be. She suspected he was softer on the inside than he appeared or than he usually showed the world.

Why would anyone want to kill him?

He turned suddenly, and she almost ran into him, getting another whiff of his tantalizing breath. She had to admit it was preferable to the biting spray Reese used. Her gaze lifted to Mark's intriguing mouth, the upper lip sculpted as if from stone by the hand of a master, the lower lip equally well defined. Would he taste as good as he smelled?

The urge to find out burned a hot streak right from her belly into her cheeks. She went tense, her hands fisting, her nails biting into her palms. She hadn't come here to taste this man, but his wares.

"I'll give Bridget a call and set up another time to meet with her, unless..." He shoved a scarred hand through his short hair. "Are you particularly concerned about the cake?"

About the cake. About my wayward urges. Yes, concerned. Confused. More than you will ever know. "Uh, no, not really."

"Because if you are, I've got all kinds of suggestions that have been very popular."

"No. I'd rather you and Bridget..." She trailed off as her gaze took in the long room that appeared both functional and cozy. Two Victorian love seats faced one another in front of a Victorian-style fireplace full of blazing logs. A work center with computer and file cabinet hugged the bay window to the front of the house, and the other end of the room that might once have been the dining room held a conference table. The only food in sight popped at her from posters framed on the walls above waist-high, built-in bookshelves.

She guessed the swinging door between the bookshelves led to the kitchen area. Though she already knew the answer, she asked, "Do you live here?"

"Upstairs. We use the lower level for storage."

"We?"

"My partners, Candee Chen and Nanette White."

"Do they live here, too?"

"No." He frowned at her, curiosity warming his eyes. "Why?"

Her stomach growled loud enough to deter his attention. Livia blushed and laughed self-consciously. "So, when do we start sampling food?"

His eyebrows danced. "I wasn't aware you expected me to provide samples tonight."

She sniffed and caught the rich aromas still prevalent in the air. "Well, something smells...wonderful."

"Ah, that's part of the chamber of commerce luncheon for tomorrow."

"You prepare it this far ahead?"

"Some dishes, yes." He glanced toward the kitchen and she heard a soft murmur of voices, punctuated by something that sounded like the bump of a lid against a pan. She'd expected they'd be alone, but maybe this wouldn't be so bad. Maybe if he were distracted by others, it would afford her the opportunity to snoop. He followed the direction of her gaze. "If you're hungry, I'm sure I can find some—"

"No, no. I'm fine. Full." She clutched the tablet to her stomach, hoping it wouldn't decide to call her a liar at that moment. "But if we aren't going to sample food tonight, then what are we doing?"

"There's a lot of paperwork to do before we get to the tasting stage."

"Paperwork? What kind of paperwork?" Suspicion lifted her eyebrows. "More contracts?"

He shook his head and suppressed a smirk. "You haven't done this before, have you?"

"Well, of course not. One marriage is quite enough, don't you think?"

The smirk dropped from his face and his gaze grew distant, sad, angry. He pressed his fists against each other as though pressing emotions back into some internal hiding place, and when he looked at her again, his expression was unreadable. "Worked with a caterer, I meant."

"Oh." She touched her hair, wondering at his secret

pain, wondering if it had anything to do with someone wanting him dead. "No, I haven't."

"Please, sit down." He motioned her toward the conference table where she spotted a legal pad and several three-ring binders with different labels like Wine, Hot Hors d' oeuvres, Cold Hors d'oeuvres, First Course, Second Course, Third Course, Desserts, Wedding Cakes. "There are a lot of decisions to make."

She eyed the binders with a silent moan. She felt her head spin.

He said, "I'll need to know what budget we're working within, what wines you'd like served, which hors d'oeuvres, whether you're having a buffet or sit-down meal. The usual." He grinned, but she wasn't amused. In fact, she felt downright dizzy. He seemed to notice. "You don't look too well. Would you rather come back tomorrow?"

"No." They didn't have enough tomorrows to put off even one evening. She shook her head adamantly, and her balance went south. She felt herself falling like a tree in a forest, but couldn't stop from crashing right into his chest.

His big arms came around her quick and strong, yet so tender she didn't feel trapped, just supported, protected, wrapped in a spice-scented blanket—safe for the first time since she'd realized her nightmare hadn't been a bad dream. How was that possible? How could being in the arms of the man whose life she would trade for her own make her feel such a sense of security?

MARK HADN'T HELD a woman since... His throat clogged at the painful memory that came rushing into his mind. He shoved it away, wishing he could shove away the warm, tender, sexy-smelling woman pressing his chest. Another time, another place, he might have relished embracing Reese Rayburn's fiancée, but right now, he just felt sorry for her, and he hated that. He didn't want to like her, to be grateful to her, to feel anything for this woman. Not even pity.

She was just a means to an end.

If he lost sight of that, he'd lose the one thing that mattered to him more than his own life. Why couldn't she have been the brainless bimbo he'd assumed Reese was marrying—instead of a drop-dead knockout with a scrumptious body, the face of an angel and the ferocity of a mother hen guarding her frightened chick?

His hand hit the bare skin at her back in that gap between her sweater and the waistband of her slacks. She didn't even flinch, but *he* did. Heat sizzled through his fingertips, raced up his arms, through his system, and into the core of him. Need, sharp and fierce, tugged at his groin.

Whoa, boy. Touching this little hottie is as dangerous as grabbing a sizzling broiler pan without oven mitts.

He led her to the conference table, sat her down, promised to be right back, then ducked into the kitchen. Nanette and Candee had gone, the food for the chamber luncheon put away, the preparations for the morning's dishes readied. He glanced at the fresh lemon twists he'd made earlier, then decided against serving pastry. Livia Kingston didn't seem the kind of woman who would appreciate being plied with high fats. He quickly put together a tray of fresh fruit, cheese and a pot of herbal tea.

She seemed to have recovered somewhat and was flipping through one of the three-ring binders. She gazed up and he read confusion in her wide aqua eyes. "I had no idea there were so many choices."

"Look, have some tea and something to eat first, okay? I'm guessing your blood sugar dropped off the charts."

She gave him a sheepish grin. "I confess. I didn't eat. I thought—well, you know what I thought."

She put a wedge of cheddar on a slice of apple and took a bite, closing her eyes, sighing noisily as though her teeth sank into nirvana. The sound, like a raw sensual moan, stroked Mark's nerves, his senses, deepened his attraction to this woman who, in so many ways, was off-limits.

And yet, every time he looked at her, he felt some weird connection, not just a male/female lure that would be natural given that he hadn't been with a woman for way too long, given that she was head-turning tasty. This felt as if he knew her on some spiritual level—which made no sense whatsoever. He'd given up believing in spiritual anything two years ago.

But whatever the lure, he couldn't deny he felt something for this woman, something more than his body's response to her, though *that* was potent enough.

He struggled against the need tightening his jeans and poured steaming tea into a mug. The tip of her pink tongue flicked out to gather in a shred of cheese from her lush bottom lip, and his control slipped again, his need building, increasing his discomfort, his chagrin.

He swore to himself, then gulped hot tea, the result exactly as expected. Pain ripped his concentration to his burned mouth, as effective an antidote as a cold shower on his engorged lust.

Until she reached out and touched him. "Are you okay?"

Hell, no, he wasn't okay. He stared at her delicate smooth-skinned hand laid on his large scarred one, and an eerie sensation swept over him, shivering up his arm and straight into his heart. He lifted his gaze to hers and saw in the depths of those enchanting aqua orbs that she felt it, too, a pre-knowledge of some sort. Nanette would probably say he'd known her in another life, but Mark didn't believe in that reincarnation crap. A shudder rattled through him, through the very depths of him, clear into his soul.

What the hell was this...this strange sense that Livia Kingston and he were somehow bonded beyond his catering her wedding for his own purposes? Beyond *her* caring for *his son, Josh?*

Chapter Five

SNEAKY PIE

Ingredients: 1 Cup Flattery
2 Cups Concession
10 Sticky Fingers
Lots of Crust

He senses it. Our connection. Livia saw it in Mark Everett's golden gaze as it locked on her with a beam as bright and delving as a police searchlight, perception dawning, riveting her to her chair, rattling her to her toes. *Not the how of it, nor the why, nor the what. Just the essence of it. The fact of it.*

He straightened in his chair, his frown deepening, his eyes narrowing on her as though he couldn't really believe it and sought her confirmation. Livia wanted to deny it, wanted to look away, but it was as if he held her face cupped in both hands.

She lifted her chin, swallowed against the knot forming in her throat. She wasn't about to enlighten him. Not until she had more information on him. On who was after him. And she was no closer to learning that than she had been two days ago. She had to get into his private area of the house. Somehow.

Seeking a distraction from his intense stare, she blurted, "Sookie Rayburn tells me your pastries are—" *Oh, God, why had she said that?* Heat soared into her cheeks as the full impact of Sookie's comments roared through her brain "—are...are to die for."

He lifted one eyebrow, obviously aware she was trying to divert his attention, but flattered nonetheless. "Would you like to *taste* my pastries...?"

"No!" Her face grew hotter. She snatched another slice of apple and cheese. "This is...is plenty—"

"Are you sure you wouldn't prefer...fresh lemon twists?"

"No, no, no thank you." She bit into the apple and cheese, speaking, chewing, pointing at the three-ring binders. "Maybe we should start on those decisions."

"Yeah, we'd better." He pulled the legal pad close and penned "Rayburn/Kingston Wedding" across the top. "What budget will we be working with?"

Livia washed the food down with a gulp of herbal tea. She'd divided the total of her savings account into categories, setting so much aside for each of the wedding expenses. She told him the amount reserved for the alcohol. "I'm paying for as much of this as I can afford on my own. My parents offered, but they're buying my dress and that's a big enough hit for them to take. Since the Rayburns expect a more upscale affair than the Kingston clan usually puts on, they are taking up the slack. But I don't want to go wild on costs."

Hearing herself prattling, she realized she was telling the man more than he needed to know and stopped short at adding that in her family whenever there was a big ceremonial get-together, all the food was prepared and served by relatives, none of whom were caterers or professional chefs.

Mark wrote the amount on his tablet.

"Oh," she said, pointing at what he'd written. "Reese is providing all the food at his cost. He says this amount will actually buy about double what it would normally cost anyone else." She stopped herself again. Why hadn't she told him that in the first place, instead of running off at the mouth? She gnawed her lower lip. "Will it be enough for about two hundred guests and a sit-down dinner?"

Mark drew a circle around the number he'd written and added the note that Rayburn was providing the food at cost. Like the man, his penmanship was bold and all but unreadable. He glanced at her. "It should be more than adequate, unless you decide to splurge on Beluga caviar or...Dom Pérignon."

His voice vibrated as he spoke, the tone striking a chord in her, dragging a shiver along her spine, a warm hum along her nerve endings. The sensation stretched into several weighted seconds as she tried puzzling her reaction to this man who was not only a mystery but a danger to her. Then, Livia realized she no longer heard noises or voices in the kitchen. She was alone with Mark Everett. Her palms dampened. Her heart raced. Her stomach pinched.

Damn. If they were alone, how would she distract him long enough to snoop through his files, his personal items, his private rooms upstairs? She wouldn't. She needed another...a better plan. Maybe if she learned something about him, got him talking about himself. "How long have you been cooking?"

"Since I was a teenager."

Since he was a teenager? Wow. She hadn't learned to cook yet.

"So, what champagne would you like to serve?" He snatched the three-ring binder labeled Wines, flopped it open, and began flipping pages of bottle displays.

Livia eyed the vast array of choices and groaned inwardly. The thought of all the decisions to be made rushed throbbing pain into her temples. "What do you suggest?"

He named the most popular champagne. "It's within your budget and still nice enough to impress the Rayburns' more…discerning guests."

"Great. We'll go with that one." Livia felt as if a small burden had been lifted with the decision, and she realized if she accepted Mark's suggestions for each choice still to be checked off his lengthy list, this could be a much easier task than anticipated. "What's next?"

It didn't go as smoothly as she'd hoped, but by the end of the next hour they had three pages of possibilities. She sighed. "At least we've narrowed it down."

"I'll prepare a few of these dishes for you and that should help finalize your decisions." He tapped the dinner options, then caught her in his golden stare again. "And, since I'm on a two-week trial, we'd best do this sooner than later."

She couldn't agree more. She nodded. "Tomorrow night?"

"Good."

She rose, clutched her tablet to her chest and slowly moved her gaze around the room, taking in the attention someone had paid to every detail, noticing touches she'd skimmed over at first glance. She smiled at Mark. "This really is an enchanting house."

He seemed pleased with the praise. "Would you like to look around?"

Oh, yes. But not only to admire the restoration. She had to learn the house's vulnerability. Her best way in without an invitation. "Please."

"The kitchen's through here." He stood, gathered the platter and tea and headed through the swinging door.

Livia hurried after him. As the door swung closed behind her, she was struck immediately by the utilitarian beauty someone had managed to evoke with the use of huge windows, chrome appliances, oak planking and granite countertops. A couple of rooms had been combined into this large space that was three times the size of any normal kitchen and sported two huge sub-zero refrigerators, a restaurant stove and oven and dishwasher, a walk-in freezer, and a pantry as large as a bedroom. "My mother would give her best cutlery to prepare a meal here."

"It's a dream for any cook." He stroked the pristine counter.

"Have you done this restoration yourself?"

He chuckled as though she'd said something funny. "Don't be fooled by the shape my hands are in. I'm an ace with a spatula, but not with a hammer. Candee's father was the contractor."

She nodded, glancing toward the large windows, but could only see her own reflection. "Do you have a private backyard?"

"Sort of." He turned on a floodlight and stepped outside with her. As in the front, this porch ran the length of the house. It was partially covered, she saw, by a balcony above. There was also a small window farther down the porch that might indicate a bathroom. Mark said, ''Mostly it's a parking lot.''

Livia eyed the backyard with purpose. It was fenced on the side that bordered the road and on the side that butted the nearest neighbor. Straight back was an alleyway and beyond that another yard, another house. The edges of the yard by the fences had high shrubs and two tall fir trees near the alley, which should keep her safe from prying eyes. There was no grass, but gravel ran between the firs and spread wide near the porch for parking. A van had been backed up against the stairs.

She could do this.

Back inside, she started toward the swinging door.

''This way.'' Mark gestured in the opposite direction and strode to the far end of the room through a second swinging door. ''The house is set up so that you can go from the foyer, into the main rooms, through the kitchen to this area, where you'll see we display the linen we provide with our services, have a public rest room and another work area. Then you can continue on to the foyer.''

She glanced around the space that she guessed might once have been the original foyer. Built-in oak shelving with glass-fronted doors held masses of tablecloths and napkins in every shade of the rainbow and more...including teal. There was another desk, a copy and fax machine, and more oak file cabinets. At the back, near the kitchen, a closed door sported a small brass sign with Washroom embossed on it, and to her right, a staircase. Her gaze went to the landing above.

Mark saw the direction of her glance and turned cool eyes on her as though he'd read her mind. ''My private area is off-limits to customers.''

"Of course." A tingle of anticipation rippled through Livia as she pulled her gaze, but not her mind, from the stairs. Yes, *that* was where she'd find the information she sought. He was too protective for it not to be there. She *had* to get up there.

And she would.

They returned to the foyer and as he reached for her jacket, Livia said, "May I use your bathroom before I take off?"

"Sure. You know where it is."

She hurried into the Washroom, a delight of oak detail and Victorian touches. She hit the faucets on the free-standing sink, then dashed to the window above the toilet. There was no screen. She opened the latch and raised the sash slightly, gratified to discover it overlooked the porch as she'd hoped, and it was large enough for her to climb through.

She eased down the sash, leaving the window unlocked. A grin spread across her face. While Mark and his partners served the chamber of commerce lunch tomorrow, Livia would be here. Snooping to her heart's content.

LIVIA WATCHED the teal-and-cream Cupid's Catering van drive off, but instead of rushing out of her car, she sat rooted, held in place by the second thoughts she'd been suffering all night and all morning. She'd been glib about snooping to her heart's content. For as much as she wanted—no, *needed*—to find out everything she could about Mark Everett, she was not a sneak by nature. In a house with eight siblings, privacy had been a valued commodity. One she respected. Revered even. She recalled the violation she'd felt when her brothers had stolen her diary and read it, then teased her at the dinner table about having a crush on Cassidy Parker, the whole family chuckling at her comparing him to a brown-haired puppy she adored, the twins chanting, "Lassie Cassie, Lassie Cassie." She'd been all of eight years old and yet the pain remained fresh.

She gnawed her bottom lip. What she planned wasn't only immoral, it was a crime. A felony. Breaking and entering. If she was caught, she'd be arrested. Thrown in jail. Reese and his family would be humiliated. The whole Kingston clan would be humiliated—as humiliated as she'd been that long-ago night.

But if she didn't do this, she would be dead in twenty-five days.

Livia shuddered. Breaking her options down to the basest level, humiliation or death, cleared her mind. She had no choice. She exited the car. The weather had gone damp and chilly, a winter storm expected by early evening. Beneath the fear gripping her senses, she caught the scent of rain in the air, felt the chill through her spandex clothing.

She wore workout clothes—the grass-green outfit that Sookie said made her look ill—figuring the color would blend in with the surrounding shrubbery as she stole to the house, that the give of the fabric would facilitate squirming through a window. But the spandex offered no protection against the damp chill. She hugged herself, then slapped at her crossed arms, her gloves making a soft *wop-wop* sound that seemed as loud as gunshot cracks to her sensitive ears.

This time of day, neighborhood businesses enjoyed moderate activity, customers and clients, buyers and browsers coming and going. Livia batted at her arms again, hopping from foot to foot, waiting for a car to pass, then crossed to the other side of the street. To most, she likely appeared to be a jogger. She doubted anyone would give her a second glance...as long as she acted like one. She sprinted into the alley behind Mark's house, arms pumping, legs scissoring as if she were out for a brisk aerobic run.

As she neared the fence, she slowed, took another glance around, alert for vigilant neighbors. Not all of these old houses had been converted to commercial enterprises. Some of the original residents refused to sell and move. As near as she could tell, no one peered out any of the windows on either side of Cupid's Catering.

Livia gathered a bracing breath and stepped onto Mark's property. The roar of an approaching vehicle on the road beside the fence jolted her. She scrambled to the closest of the two pine trees and pressed herself against the trunk, trying to make herself small. Invisible. The prickly bark bit through the spandex, jabbing her flesh, scarring the fabric. She held her breath, swallowing a groan of discomfort.

The car passed without turning into the alley. She eased away from the tree and exhaled in relief...until her gaze swept the back of the house. In the daylight, she could see the same attention to detail had been paid to the outside restoration as to the inside. It was an impressive house, and at the moment, a foreboding one. The windows seemed like large black eyes, flat, lifeless; the eyes of a sleeping monster.

A monster she was about to awaken?

She swallowed hard over the ridiculous thought and made herself move. Her hands were starting to sweat inside her gloves, her skin no longer felt chilled. Adrenaline had her blood zinging, her nerves alive, but she knew that once the rush vanished, so would this spurt of energy.

Thank goodness she didn't have to return to work. She'd told Jane, her boss at the gym, that she was having a root canal and Jane had insisted she take off for the rest of the day.

Livia climbed to the porch, so nervous she hopped up the stairs two at once, the hourglass bumping her chest, reminding her of the urgency, the necessity. *In and out.* She had to get in and out. At the most, she probably had two hours. She glanced at her watch. One hour and forty-five minutes now. Time was wasting.

She scurried to the bathroom window. It was higher than she'd realized looking out last night, the sill coming just below her shoulders. She needed to stand on something to hoist herself inside. She glanced around, spotted a grouping of patio chairs and individual folding tables. She decided one of the tables would do and propped it in place.

It was solid plastic and sturdy enough to hold her weight, but as she balanced gingerly on it, it occurred to her that Mark or one of his partners could have discovered the unlocked window and locked it. Her stomach dipped. She reached up, pressed her gloved palms to the glass and shoved upward on the sash. The window didn't move.

"No, no, no." She grunted with new effort, and this time the window eased open. She glanced over her shoulder once more, then stood stock-still, listening for any unexpected noises inside the house. Nothing. With the agility that made her one of Jane's best aerobic instructors, Livia lifted one leg onto the sill, then pulled herself up by the window frame and slid in the other leg. She arched her back and inched downward, feeling the unseeable area below her with the tip of her shoe.

She heard the splash at the same time she felt the

water closing over her foot. The toilet. Damn. Obviously a man had used it last. The seat was up. Groaning, she flicked the lid closed with her dry foot, then settled her full weight on it, fighting the slippery slide of her sole.

Hunched over, she stepped to the floor, one foot raised, and grabbed the hand towel from the brass ring. She dried her foot and the floor. At least the water hadn't penetrated the leather. But it had turned the towel and her shoe blue. Great. She closed the window and rolled the towel into a ball. A laundry room hadn't been on the tour last night, but with all that linen in the storage shelves and what they had to use in the kitchen, there must be one. Unless…they used a laundry service. She huffed out a breath. That's probably what they did. But Mark lived here. There might be a washer and dryer somewhere.

She crept to the door, put her ear to the wood and listened hard. She heard nothing and eased the door open inch by inch. The hourglass seemed to thump, urging her to hurry. Hurry. She stepped into the area with the linen and staircase and froze. Music wafted through the house. A radio or CD playing somewhere. Livia's heart rate rose. Was someone in the house? She stayed perfectly still, straining to hear any other noises, something that would announce another's presence.

Nothing. She sneaked to the door that led into the kitchen and cracked it just enough to see through. No one. She felt the tension ease from her shoulders. Her folks always left a radio on when they weren't home. It wasn't a farfetched idea that Mark and his crew had done the same, or even left it on by mistake. She had to get upstairs and then get out of here.

She raced to the stairs before she lost her nerve. She

climbed quickly, her heart hammering in her chest. The scrape of a chair against planked floor resounded from somewhere in the house and halted her ascent halfway up. *Dear God, someone was here. Coming this way.* Livia glanced up, then down. She couldn't make it back to the bathroom. The only place to hide was in Mark's private quarters. She scrambled to the landing and reached for his door.

Oh, please don't let it be locked.

Chapter Six

SECRET SAUCE

Take One Snoop
Add One Liar
Get: An Old Family Recipe

No matter how hard he tried, Mark Everett couldn't wrench Livia Kingston from his mind. He'd spent the night tossing and turning, her cherubic face filling the space behind his closed, sleepless eyelids, his body aching with a long unfulfilled need that she had stirred with a vengeance. The need he understood. The woman he did not.

How could she be engaged to a jerk like Reese? Could she actually be in love? Maybe it was the Rayburn money. Or the prestige the Rayburn name offered. Was she a gold digger? A social climber? Somehow he could not put either of those together with the woman he'd seen gleefully playing soccer with a little boy.

On so many levels, she puzzled him, but most of all, he didn't understand that spooky moment of connection he'd felt with her. It had been more than an awareness, more than attraction, more than long-denied lust.

By dawn he'd concluded Livia Kingston was a distraction he could not afford. He had to remember that and not allow her to steer him from his course. He was too close to grasping the prize.

Wind sent a spume of rain against the windshield of the van. His grip tightened on the steering wheel, his patience thinning at the caution of drivers ahead of him. *God, you'd think slick, wet streets were a rarity in western Washington.* He cursed. His patience as thin as crepe. He had to get back to the house and start the dishes he'd planned to tempt Ms. Kingston with tonight and send Candee back to the hall to help Nanette serve the chamber members dessert, and handle the cleanup and packing up afterward.

But he had another destination first and if he didn't get there within the next couple of minutes... Damn. It took all of his restraint to keep from slamming his foot on the gas pedal and making a bad situation worse. But the urge to do exactly that didn't ease until he pulled across from the front of the building where Josh attended kindergarten class and saw the children spilling out.

A flash of red caught his eye—Josh's jacket. Mark's heart gave a kick. The boy's sandy hair stuck up in the exact spot on his forehead as Wendy's had. God, he looked so much like her. And he was getting so tall. So quickly. His throat tightened with regret and the anger that seemed always to simmer beneath the surface. He'd missed two years of his son's life. Years he could not retrieve.

A wet gust of wind struck the boy and his jacket flapped open like a cape, plastering his T-shirt to his ribs. Mark eyed him with a father's keen assessment and felt a new rage. Though he was getting taller, Josh seemed too thin. Was no one paying the least attention to his diet? His appetite? Was he ill? If he wasn't, the way the rain soaked through his clothes, he would be.

He fought the impulse to jump from the van and to race to zip up the boy's jacket. Fought it hard. He had no right to know anything or to do anything about his son. Yet. It was a choice Mark had made. For good cause. He had to find what he was after. Irrefutable proof. *Before* he thrust himself back into his child's life. He could not, would not, risk putting that kid through any extra pain.

But oh, God, this hurt, this ache to hold Josh, to stroke back his cowlick, to tuck him into bed at night, to play ball with him, to listen to his endless chatter, his endless questions.

The boy caught sight of a long black car, and his small hand went up in the air as he ran toward it like a miniature business man flagging down a cab. A pint-size Reese in the making. Mark growled. The limousine driver held the back door open, and Josh scrambled inside. Mark choked on resentment. Where was Livia Kingston? Why wasn't she picking up the boy today? Or Reese? Or Sookie? Someone besides a damned paid servant? He cursed, his fist slamming the steering wheel. This was no existence for a kid.

Mark could barely swallow the frustration jamming his throat, the utter helplessness as he had to sit there and watch the long black car drive off. "Soon. Soon, Josh."

He started the van and headed home, more determined than ever to please Livia Kingston the only way he knew, by seducing her with food.

He *would* cater her wedding.

By the time he arrived home the day had gone as dark as his mood, the storm raging like his emotions. He backed the van up to the stairs outside the kitchen and locked it. Once he'd been a trusting soul, the kind of guy who left his keys in his car. No more. Caution and precaution were his mantras these days. Struggling to set aside his frustrations about Josh and not caring that the rain soaked through his clothing, he studied the back of the house as he climbed the porch.

In prison he'd discovered the value of observation, of sensing something amiss in the very air. It was a lesson hard learned, at much personal expense. He rubbed the back of his scarred hand, tapped what remained of his original God-given nose, his God-given jaw.

A *clunk-clunk* caught his attention. One of the patio tables lay on its side beneath the bathroom window, colliding with the house on every gust of wind. He caught it and put it back where it belonged, wondering how it had escaped from between the chairs. Not the wind. More likely the gust that moved this was human.

He scanned the alleyway, the area beside the tree, rain slashing into his eyes. He no longer expected the best from his fellow man. He'd been naive once, but now he knew most people were capable of crimes the average Joe never suspected.

He saw no one, but if someone *was* out there, he hoped to hell they got drenched.

Wiping at his face with his sleeve, he turned toward the back door and stepped into the kitchen. He took a deep breath, feeling welcomed by the lingering scents of spices and sauces, the sense of sanity afforded him in this room by its pristine coolness, its homey chaos, its sources of creation. All the big and small appliances that allowed him to practice the one thing he had any feel for. The thing he'd been denied while behind bars.

He stroked the granite countertop. He owed Candee and Nanette more than he could ever repay them. After his arrest he could count his friends on one hand without using all of his fingers. He bit down that aging hurt and embraced instead his luck at having made a few true friendships.

Candee and Nanette had stuck by him, believed in his innocence, and aided in his re-establishing a new life when his lawyer discovered he had never been read his rights at the time of his arrest. This violation of his fourth amendment rights had provided the means of overturning his sentence. At the time, he'd feared the Rayburns and the press would descend on him like vultures seeking to finish their prey. But he wasn't even sure if the Rayburns knew. Thanks to an exploding sex scandal involving the governor, the Ethan Marshall release dwindled to page ten news. The small article was accompanied by an old photograph, one taken before Mark had gone to jail.

So, here he was. A free man. Lucky to have a few good friends who'd believed in him and his talents enough to secure loans for the restoration of this house and provide the starter cash that had set their business on its feet.

Of course, it was also self-serving. As his partners, they shared in the profit. But he was using his share to pay off the loans, to purchase the house.

"Ah, Big E, you're dripping wet." Candee came through the swinging door, his jet-black hair combed smooth off his flat face and caught at the nape in a leather thong. His smile narrowed his eyes to slits. "I guess I'd better wear my slicker."

"I'd recommend it." Mark shook rain from his head and hands, noticing for the first time the discomfort of wet cotton clinging to his upper body. He tossed him the keys to the van. "Nanette is waiting for you to show up with that flan, buddy."

"It's ready. I can't believe I dropped the tray this morning." He glanced around the spotless kitchen. "Took me an hour to clean up the mess."

"Stuff happens. Speaking of which, did you hear anything on the porch while you were working at the computer?"

"No." He gave a sheepish grin. "But I was listening to a new CD. Rather loudly. Is something wrong?"

"Nah. Just a displaced patio table."

Candee shrugged into his parka. "Ah, the wind... Perhaps we should not have set the patio furniture out this early."

"Perhaps." Mark didn't believe for a minute that the wind had moved that table, but he left his fears unvoiced. Candee had had enough upset for one day. But as he watched his partner move to the refrigerator, he couldn't resist ribbing him. "You need help with the flan?"

"You wound me." Candee laughed as he pulled the covered tray from the middle shelf. "I'll be extra careful with this batch."

As soon as Candee pulled away, Mark locked the back door. Despite the fact he loathed being locked in, he *had* to lock the world out. Candee and Nanette wanted a security system, but Mark couldn't stand cops, even rent-a-cops, showing up at his doorstep.

They'd compromised, putting his sensitivities over their own. Something else he owed them for.

He'd installed dead bolts and other secure locks that required his personal inspection. He went through the house now, checking the kitchen, dining room, showroom and foyer, finding every lock engaged. The first irregularity he encountered was at the washroom. Company policy charged the door be shut at all times. It stood ajar. Had Candee left it open amid his distress over the spilled flan? Or did the table outside this window indicate something more sinister?

With the hair on his nape prickling, he pushed the door inward. The room was empty. Breath rushed from him on a laugh. He crossed to the window. Unlocked. His humor fled. He studied the room a long moment, then realized the brass towel ring lacked its guest towel, and a blue mark—the exact color of the stuff Nanette used to keep the bowl clean—adorned the oak toilet lid. He peered at it. Almost an outline. Like the edge of...of a shoe?

He glanced up at the window and his nerves chattered. Had someone stolen in through that window? Wouldn't Candee have heard someone in the house? He considered. Then decided with a CD playing loud and the cacophony of thunder and wind for accompaniment, he might not have.

On the other hand, maybe he was jumping to conclusions. There were other explanations. Less nefarious ones. He should have asked Candee whether or not he'd had any customers this morning. Someone with a child, perhaps.

But as a precaution, he returned to the kitchen, gathered an iron skillet for a weapon, then went down to the cellar and found it secure. The only other place someone could be was upstairs in his private quarters, but no respectable thief would find anything there worth the price of admission. In fact, if someone was up there, what they were about to encounter was one pissed off chef, wet and cold, who wanted nothing more than privacy and a hot shower. Gripping the pan by the handle, he moved up the steps with unusual caution, and silently swung the door open.

This upper level divided into four rooms. No hard-wood planking up here, but wall-to-wall carpet...for his son's comfort. Plus, he figured it would mute any noise a child's footfalls might make. Thinking to bring the outdoors indoors, he'd chosen to do the whole of his living quarters in shades of green with yellow accents, and a dinosaur theme.

The main area stretched the width of the house and held his exercise equipment—one of those Bowflex machines that bolted to the wall—a boom box, a recliner and a nineteen-inch TV with built-in VCR. There was also a full bathroom and two bedrooms, the largest reserved for Josh.

Mark approached the bathroom and bumped open the door. It appeared to be as he'd left it. The hand towel rumpled, the shower curtain bunched at one end of the claw-footed tub. He peeked behind the door. No one. He moved on to Josh's room. Dreaded going in. Made himself. Without the boy, it seemed more of a monument to a kid than a kid's room. He stood in the center of it. Studying it. The trucks and train set appeared unmoved. The books untouched. The bedspread unruffled. His frustration over Josh struck with renewed vengeance and Mark crossed to the closet, yanked it open. It was empty. He hadn't bought the boy any clothes. Didn't know his size.

Pain pressed his heart, digging deep through the un-healed fissure that had ripped through him that atrocious night two years ago.

He checked under the bed, then rushed out, closing the door as if *that* could lock away the hurt and pain he couldn't ease.

He approached his own room with revived caution, bumping the door open with the toe of his shoe. His gaze went immediately to the bed—the sheets half on and half off in testament to his restless night.

Livia Kingston's image filled his mind and he smacked the skillet against his palm. Damn that woman. She *would* get into his head. He stormed to his closet, slapped open the door. Nothing. He plowed his hand through his clothes. No one hiding at the back. He knelt and checked under his bed. Nobody.

"You're all alone, buddy." He sighed at the cold, harsh truth of how very alone he was, put the skillet down on his bed, got a bath towel from the linen closet, then stripped off his wet clothes. With the towel wrapped at his waist, he stalked to the bathroom and lathered his face. Shaved. Then he reached behind the shower curtain, turned on the shower full blast and dropped the towel.

THE BLAST OF WATER drenched Livia. She yowled, leaping from behind the dinosaur shower curtain. Water dripped from her hair into her eyes and her clothes cleaved her body like wet paint, accentuating every feminine curve and crevice. But compared to the naked man gaping at her, she felt wrapped in blankets.

Mark Everett's expression ran the gambit from shocked to pissed in half seconds, but his fury was lost on her as her gaze locked on his body. *Dear God, he was gorgeous.* His shoulders wide enough for a woman to feel protected in his embrace, the raven hair dappling his molded chest looking silken enough to tease a woman's fingertips, his belly as hard as a rocky river-bed, and the prize package lower definitely worth taking off the ribbon to enjoy. She blushed, jerked her head up and met the fire of his golden eyes.

Mark's heart galloped inside his chest as he glared at the drenched woman standing in his tub, her streaked-blond hair plastered to her head, her aqua eyes wide—not so much with shock but something…darker, sensual, definitely breath-stealing. His gaze wandered over her breasts, lingered on her erect nipples, probed the cleft between her legs. It was as if his dreams of her had caused her to materialize. He felt the heat reach into him, rouse him.

She noticed and yelped. He bent to grab the towel at his feet. She jumped from the bathtub and darted past him, out the door. Securing the towel, he raced after her. Tackled her. Pulled her beneath him. They were nose to nose, but she didn't scream as he'd expected. "What the hell are you doing here?"

"Let me up! Now!" Her hands slammed against his arms, his face.

He grabbed her wrists and pinned them over her head. He felt her struggling beneath him, felt his body responding to the enticing movements, fought against it. "Why did you climb through my bathroom window and hide up here?"

Her eyes narrowed with defiance. "Who…who are you?"

Her question started his heart thundering harder and harder. Had she figured it out? Did she know? He stared deep into her eyes. Something sharp poked his breastbone, something she was wearing, a necklace maybe, and—as though it were a magical key, it seemed to unlock and reveal that strange connection he'd felt the night before with Livia Kingston.

What did it mean? What?

She gulped. "What are…are you going to do to me?"

Mark blinked, realizing he was fully aroused, his need pressing hard against the wet cloth gloving her belly, her beaded nipples jabbing his chest. She didn't seem to feel the fear inherent in her question. In fact, her eyes shone with something like curiosity, like need. He stroked one of her rock-hard nipples, then began moving his hand over her belly and lower. "What would you like me to do?"

His gaze locked on to her mouth, and she licked her lips, quit struggling, puckering slightly as if challenging him silently to do what he wanted more than anything: to kiss her. He obliged, lowering his mouth to hers, tasting her. He released her wrists and she moaned, her hands moving into his hair, her lips going pliant, then hungry.

His need leapt degrees higher.

His conscience gnawed at him, shouting about the thin line he walked between acting on the fire raging through his veins and what was right. Livia Kingston would distract him. He pulled away from her and stood, gathering the towel around himself as if his erection were not visible to them both. "I'm not the one who was hiding in *your* bathroom, Ms. Kingston. You ought to consider yourself fortunate that I don't thrust myself on women who don't want me."

Livia's breath puffed out of her. Her face flared as red as ripe tomatoes. Embarrassment. Humiliation. Or mortification. The air between them seemed to sizzle. To crackle. She might regret what had just happened. Might want to deny she'd felt anything. But she hated that he knew she'd been as swept up in that kiss as he had.

She stumbled up and backed away from him, fingering her kiss swollen lips. "Why do you have a photograph of Josh's family on your chest of drawers? Who are you?"

Mark pointed toward the door. "Get out."

"I will find out." Livia spun and left, running down the stairs as if he were chasing her.

But Mark couldn't move. Fear shivered from his brain to the soles of his bare feet, nailing him to the floor. Fear that she would do exactly what she claimed.

And that would ruin everything.

Chapter Seven

STEAMED AND CLAMMY

Lots of Chicken Soup
Equal Parts: Soul Searching
Fact Finding
Serve with New Perspective

"Are you feeling any better, dear?" Bev Kingston's face was inches from Livia's nose.

Her red, runny nose.

She had lost a week, seven whole days of her precious remaining twenty-five, laid out by the worst cold—or coldlike flu virus—she had ever suffered. Every muscle in her body ached. Her head felt heavy, as though it was stuffed with packing peanuts made of lead; she could barely lift it off the pillow.

Her mother held a cupped palm beneath a spoon, bringing broth toward Livia's mouth. "I've fixed you my special chicken soup. You really should try and eat some. A couple of sips at least."

Livia groaned and tried raising up enough to take in the liquid without spilling it down her chin. The warm broth rolled over her tongue and into her throat. She knew immediately that she was nowhere near being well. Her mother made prize-winning chicken soup, but what she'd just swallowed had no taste.

"I really think you should let me call Dr. Smith." Bev looked worried. "You haven't been running a temperature this whole time, but, honestly, you're as pale as eggshells, have lost what little appetite you had, and don't seem to be getting any better."

"I am better, Mom, honest." But the lie laid heavy against her heart and hearing the list of symptoms, Livia began wondering whether she actually had a virus or if she'd contracted this "illness" to run away from the mess her life was in, to hide from truths she refused to face, from things she couldn't figure out.

She glanced toward the flowers Reese had sent, a single bunch of roses, the same pink as the bedroom trimmings, the petals wilting now, withering. Like her? Was she ill? Or was her subconscious trying to protect her? The possibility wasn't that farfetched. If she stayed in bed the next three weeks, she would stay alive, stay out of the line of fire of that fatal bullet.

Would not see that fatal bullet take Mark Everett's life.

Shying away from the horror of *that,* she accepted another sip of soup from her mother, closing her eyes as she swallowed. Her mother dabbed her chin with a napkin, but Livia sensed it more than felt it, her mind absorbed elsewhere—back at the night she'd searched the caterer's living quarters, which had been more of a surprise than a revelation. She'd expected a typical bachelor pad, like those of past boyfriends, but Mark Everett's personal abode resembled the residence of a single father, child's room and all. Except he had no child. If he did, there would have been clothing in the closet, in the dresser. Granted, there had been a few toys but none that appeared to ever have been played with.

And why did he have a framed photograph of Josh, Wendy and Ethan Marshall?

He'd refused to tell her.

Left her to figure it out for herself, and instead she'd run straight home into this bed, where she'd stayed ever since.

She accepted another spoonful of soup.

"I hope you aren't fretting about your wedding preparations, dear. Things are getting handled," her mother said. "Reese's mother has some wonderful ideas for the flowers and says not to fret if she exceeds your budget. She'll cover any extras. Your daddy and I have the invitations almost ready for mailing, and Bridget and that nice Mr. Everett have been busy designing your wedding cake."

Livia choked, spewing the soup. "Mark Everett has been meeting with Bridget?"

"Yes." Her mother mopped at her chin, her neck, and the bedding. "And oh, what a cake it will be. Too beautiful to eat."

"Good," Livia mumbled. Just the thought of cake set her stomach churning. Or was it that damned man who had her on edge? He had nerve, she would give him that. More than she did. She'd figured after their last encounter... *Oh, God, their last encounter.* Memories flooded back and smeared her cheeks with heat. Memories that included his beautiful body. His beautiful, naked body. His beautiful, naked, aroused body.

And her reaction to it.

The same flash of awakening arousal she'd felt then exploded through her now. She fought the sensation.

Didn't want to feel it. But she knew it was one thing to tell herself that she still had the right to look at the opposite sex when the mood struck, that she was a healthy sexual being who was only betrothed, not dead—and quite another to find her whole body tingling with awareness for a man other than her fiancé; to find herself so curious about that man's kiss that she'd allowed—no, invited—his passion; to respond to that man's kiss with a hunger she had never experienced with Reese, never even dreamed she could feel.

No. She did not want to be attracted to Mark Everett. Not only was he a complete mystery, he was far too dangerous to her on every imaginable level. Livia touched her lips, recalling the disturbing, illicit kiss and knew it was too late. She was already attracted to him.

With this admission came a decrease in the pounding at her temples, as though the lead-packing peanuts in her head had evolved into feathers.

"Oh, I forgot to tell you," Bev said, "the bridal shop called. They need your decision about the wedding gown Bridget and I put on hold for you."

The slinky satin, off-the-shoulder, plain-Jane dress that Mark Everett's hot golden gaze had made her feel downright sinful wearing. How could she marry Reese wearing a dress that would always remind her of Mark? How could she marry Reese if Mark were killed on the eve of her wedding?

Should she be marrying Reese?

She glanced again at the withering flowers he'd sent. One bunch. No more. Another man might have filled her sickroom with bouquets. Another man might have called day and night to check on her. As far as she knew, Reese had called three times in seven days, fewer times than her employer and co-workers.

She ought to feel hurt. Or angry. Or something more than slighted. But she didn't, and that made her wonder whether she had the kind of love for her fiancé that would sustain years of marriage. She squinted at her mother, who was fussing with her pillows, straightening her blankets. Her parents had enjoyed a long relationship, and they still seemed not merely content like some of her friends's parents, but actually happy, as though one needed the other to feel complete.

She had never felt "complete" with Reese. And that was all right with her. Being an extension of another person seemed like an old-fashioned way of looking at life. Of living life. Something from her parents' era, their generation. She was of a whole new generation. This was a whole new century. It required a whole new mind-set.

Didn't it?

Two weeks ago she'd have answered a resounding "Yes!" to that question. Two weeks ago she hadn't met Mark Everett. Hadn't felt the way he made her feel. Even now, as weak as a battered kitten, just thinking of him roused a honeyed ache deep in the core of her. She moaned, mortified that she lusted after a man who was not her future hus—

Her future anything.

He had no future.

She should call off the wedding.

The thought seemed to slough away another layer of the mysterious virus. Livia actually felt...hungry. "I'd like more of that soup, Mom."

Bev's blue eyes brightened. "I'll be right back with a fresh bowl and some saltines."

Livia sat up, allowing her mother to prop pillows at her back. *I don't want to marry Reese. Dear God. It was true*…and it accounted for why she'd been dragging her feet with the wedding preparations and decisions. Why she hadn't had every detail planned months ago. Then why had she accepted his ring? Agreed to become his wife? The answer seemed to have been there all the time, tucked into a corner of her mind, had she bothered to look. She was a levelheaded, plan-for-the-future woman. And Reese had stormed into her world like a white knight, offering her a life she could chart years in advance. He had security beyond her wildest hopes. He was handsome. He seemed to like children.

But did he really? She considered his disregard for Josh and realized that lately she'd been seeing the tarnish on her knight's shining armor. Maybe that was the trouble. Was Reese wearing armor of some sort?

And what of Josh? Her feelings for the boy were not in doubt; he'd burrowed into her heart on their first meeting. There had been no resisting those huge hazel eyes, that sad little face. If she didn't marry Reese, he would be hurt. But if she married Reese only to make Josh happy, they could all end up miserable.

As her mother hustled from the room, Livia twisted her two-carat engagement ring, tugged it to her knuckle, considered pulling it off, warming to the idea of canceling the wedding. If she returned Reese's ring, events would be altered. She wouldn't be shot. If she wasn't getting married, she wouldn't need a wedding caterer. Could squelch this insane attraction to that walking dead man once and for all.

The hourglass vibrated between her breasts. She grabbed hold of the chain and pulled it from beneath her sleep shirt. Her gaze landed on the demarcation lines. *Eighteen days.* A life sentence. For her? Or for

Mark? No matter where she turned, or what she did, Livia could not run and hide from the fact that if she lived, he died. Shivers racked her. She buried her face in her hands, but couldn't vanquish the unbidden image of that gorgeous man with a gaping, bleeding hole in his incredible chest. There had to be another way.

There had to be.

Shock ran the length of her. When had her instinct for self-preservation been diluted by concern for a man she didn't even know? Or trust? A man Heaven expected to accept into its fold in eighteen days? How had she managed to let herself care as much about Mark Everett losing his life as she cared about losing her own?

She shook her head, torment tightening her chest. Maybe the alternative she sought was not in how to prevent herself from getting shot but in how to keep them *both* from getting shot.

The hourglass tingled again and her mind's eye filled with the Processor's face—stern with disapproval. His voice filled her head—thick with reprimand, warning her to leave well enough alone. To concentrate on saving her own skin. To attend to the job for which she'd been given this second chance.

As much as Livia wanted to live out the sixty-odd years allotted her in the Processor's computer, how could she stand by and allow someone to shoot Mark Everett? She'd been raised to respect human life. If she could save him as well as herself, she had to try.

She inhaled with both nostrils, the air sliding through without interruption, the stuffiness amazingly gone. She stretched, ran her hands through her matted hair. Once she filled her belly, she would take a long hot shower, check her e-mail and head to the library to start what she should have started seven days ago: looking into Mark's connection to Josh's parents.

The rattle of plates and silverware alerted her to her mother's imminent arrival, and shifted her mind to her own parents, her own family and Reese's family. Livia cringed. How in the world she would break the news to everyone that she was calling off the wedding they'd been working so hard to pull together for her.

In the end she decided *that* bad news could wait a while longer. She had other, more pressing matters to tend to first. She ate, showered, dressed and read her e-mail, which consisted of a few "get well" wishes, forwarded jokes and cyber ads. Nothing from Chad. He and a couple of his computer-savvy pals were doing their own checking into Mark Everett's background. If there was something to find, they would unearth it.

Livia set out into the midmorning, wrapped in her hooded raincoat against a driving downpour. If she was going to find Mark's connection to Josh's parents, she needed to know more about Wendy Marshall's murder and Ethan Marshall's arrest and prosecution than what she could learn from newspaper accounts. But it was a place to start, would give her some basic information before she began to subtly question Reese and his family.

Two years had passed since Josh's father had been sent to prison for life. She hadn't known Reese while his family had gone through this tragedy. Of course, she'd seen the media frenzy—couldn't have escaped hearing about it if she'd wanted to—but she'd given the whole mess little attention. At the time, she'd just been dumped by Turk the Jerk and had been stupidly running short on pity for anyone but herself.

She'd thought by getting engaged to Reese she'd

finally gotten over falling for the wrong kind of man. Rain pounded the roof of her car like a sitcom audience stomping its feet and hooting over a hilarious joke. This joke was on her. She'd finally realized she didn't love the one man who should be right for her, while being irresistibly attracted to a man sentenced to die in less than three weeks. "God, I'm as pathetic as this lousy day."

Strange though, even *that* realization couldn't squelch her mood, and she laughed at herself, wondering if she laughed in lieu of crying.

She merged with traffic on Front Street. "Concentrate, Livia. What do you know about the Marshalls?"

What *did* she know? She'd been going with Reese for six months, been engaged to him for the past three, and yet, all she'd really gleaned from her fiancé was that he'd loved his sister and hated her husband. Under the circumstances, she could hardly blame him, but this was not the kind of information that would help her ferret out Mark Everett's connection with the family. Trouble was, she had no idea what would help.

But this was as good a starting point as any. She pulled into the library parking lot. She wanted to refresh her mind, review those newspaper accounts that she'd given short shrift two years ago. Hoping she wouldn't have to drive to downtown Bellevue or Seattle to the offices of the local newspapers, she would try the library archives first. She edged the car into a narrow space.

She shut off the engine and glanced through the sheet of pouring rain, spotted patrons running from vehicles to the building, and vice versa, beneath what little cover they received from umbrellas or newspapers or even books they'd borrowed. She wrapped her raincoat around her, pulled up the hood, and dashed inside.

All available computers were engaged, but the young man manning the information desk told her the records she sought had yet to be put into the library's computer files and were still on microfiche.

As HE WATCHED LIVIA from across the room, the young man at the information desk dialed a certain phone number. "You said to let you know if someone showed any interest in the Ethan and Wendy Marshall case. Is it still worth a thousand dollars to you?"

"Depends on who is showing the interest."

"Livia Kingston."

Livia? Anxious fingers curled tighter around the handset. What was she doing digging into Wendy's death?

This definitely needed pursuing. "Thank you for letting me know. The thousand is yours."

Minutes later, the killer sat in the library lot, still trying to figure out how to discern what Livia wanted with information concerning Wendy's murder, when a Cupid's Catering van pulled into the next parking slot. The driver glanced toward his rearview mirror as he backed in, and a sudden flash of lightning illuminated his face.

The killer felt struck through with the jagged bolt of electricity, seared to the heart, burned to the core.

Golden eyes.

Ethan Marshall's eyes.

The killer was the only one in the Rayburn inner circle who knew Ethan had been released from prison, but since he'd made no attempted to reclaim his son, had assumed Ethan was gone, skipped town to avoid persecution, or moved to another state.

But now it was clear that he'd only changed his name and his exterior appearance. The damned newspapers hadn't bothered getting a new photograph of him. The killer had assumed he looked the same. What a stupid mistake.

And all this time, he was right under their noses, wheedling his way back into their social circles. There could be only one reason for that: he wanted to know why his bitch of a wife had had to die, wanted to know who had done the honors.

The killer watched Mark Everett rush to meet Livia at her car and shuddered with fury. And fear. The loaded gun felt cold and heavy and deadly. It was time that pompous chef joined his dearly departed. And maybe Livia, too.

MARK EVERETT would have given a thousand dollars to clear from his memory banks his last view of Livia Kingston's tight little butt swishing down his stairs, to erase the threat of her last words. He'd spent the week jumping every time the phone rang, the doorbell. He had to know whether or not she'd told anyone what she knew. Had to find out what she knew.

But according to her mother and sister, Livia was down with the flu. Had been down with the flu since the afternoon she'd run from his house. Seven excruciatingly cruel days and nights.

But today she'd recovered and come here. Why the library? Something to do with the wedding? Or something else?

His gut told him something else.

He backed the van into a slot that gave him a direct

view of the library entrance and shut off the engine. The tick of the cooling motor joined the heavy rain in making a jarring chorus of noise against his thoughts. He watched Livia hurry inside and kept his gaze glued to the door. Each minute seemed like an hour and he warred with himself against staying put or following her. As much as he wanted to speak with her, he dare not confront her in a public place. Not without knowing what she might say. Or do. Not with his control slipping as fast as the water streaming through the streets.

He sighed and shoved his hands through his hair, glued his gaze to the library door and willed her to appear. Instead she appeared in his mind, the way she'd looked with her wet clothes hugging every ripe curve of her lean body, the way she'd felt squirming beneath him, those big aqua eyes drinking him in, hinting at a passion that begged for release, and the taste of her mouth, the blood-boiling sensation of her tongue stroking his. He moaned as a spontaneous flame lit in his belly.

Damn it. It was bad enough that she distracted him, drove him to the edge and back of sexual frustration, but she was a danger to him in far worse ways. He had to prevent her from ruining everything, but how? If she was as thoroughly encamped on Reese's side of this issue as she had to be, he was doomed. Josh was doomed.

He slapped the steering wheel. *No!* Defeatism was for losers. He might once have been such a man, but not now. *If you don't control a situation, it controls you.* For him to learn that lesson, his son had paid too dear a price. He would not bring more pain down on Josh.

A flash of bright blue appeared in the library door. Mark straightened, tensed. *Yes, it was her.*

Livia dashed into the rain and sprinted for her car. He left the van and raced toward her, rain pelting him. But she seemed oblivious to it. In fact, for someone who'd been laid up with the flu all week, she seemed full of spit and vinegar. He met her at her car just as she poked the key into the lock.

She jerked back, her eyes going wide. Her face was pale, but even wet with rain, she was lovely. He resisted the urge to touch her cheek, to stroke it dry, resisted because of the fear he sensed in her tense stance. She was afraid. Of him. His ever-simmering anger boiled over. Damn it to hell. "We need to talk. Now."

"Oh, yeah?" She turned and unlocked the car door. Wrenched it open, started to scramble inside, then squared her shoulders and glared up at him. "Are you going to tell me the truth...about who you are and...and...and why you *have* to cater my wedding?"

"Yes."

She studied his face as though trying to discern whether he was lying. But he was being as honest as he knew how. While he'd waited for her to emerge from the library he'd realized the truth was his only hope. He had to level with her...for Josh's sake. His gaze locked with hers and that crazy inexplicable connection he felt to her gripped him harder than either previous time. It wasn't false. It wasn't something he'd imagined. It was there. But he didn't understand it.

"I'll tell you whatever you want to know, if you'll tell me why I feel somehow connected to you. And don't deny it, because I can see you feel the connection, too."

She blanched as if what she had to tell him was worse than what he had to tell her. Mark's gut clenched, and he knew he wasn't going to like what he was about to hear.

Chapter Eight

SPILLED BEANS

Take some:
He said
She said
Heat to Boiling
Watch Out for Flying Objects

Things are not going according to plan. Livia felt the hourglass vibrate against her heart and amended the thought to "things were not going according to *her* plan." *She* had figured she'd do some homework before confronting this man. *Heaven* and *he* seemed to have their own agendas.

She blinked against the driving rain, peering out from under her protective hood. He'd startled her, made her afraid; she realized now that the fear wasn't *of* him. But *for* him.

"Okay, but if we're going to talk it has to be somewhere private," she said. What she had to tell him was definitely for his ears only.

"And dry." He shook rain from his hair, shrugged it from his distressed leather jacket, but beaded droplets clung to his ebony lashes, giving him an irresistible vulnerability. "Warm even."

"Warm and dry." She hugged herself, more for protection against that vanilla-scented charm of his than from the weather. "Where?"

"My house?" He tilted his head as though gesturing in that general direction. "No one's there at the moment…and won't be for several hours."

She shivered at the thought of returning to the scene of their carnal encounter. She wasn't sure she trusted herself alone with him. There. "Will it take *several* hours?"

"That depends." His tawny gaze was as unyielding as a lion's stare. "On you."

On her? What did that mean? Was he going to level with her…or play sexual tag? No. That look wasn't sensual…not in any way. Whatever was going on with him had nothing to do with what had happened between them last week. She was the one with the inappropriate thoughts. The one who couldn't banish the image of his naked body, couldn't kill the memory of his touch, his taste, his kiss. *I don't thrust myself on women who don't want me.* Trouble was, she did want him. Wanted him so much her blood was alive with the need.

"Okay." She tore her gaze from his. "I'll meet you there."

As she drove to Cupid's Catering, she wondered how she would tell Mark about their "connection."

What if she couldn't find the right words?

What if he didn't believe her?

What if he did?

Livia's breath came shuddering out. What if he

couldn't be saved from his fate, even if he knew that fate ahead of time?

She parked behind the cream-and-teal van and sat staring out through the rain. Maybe she shouldn't have acceded so quickly to meeting him here. Maybe she should go somewhere and read the pages in her purse, then come back. She reached for the keys, but realized she was too late. He was signaling from the porch. She gathered a bracing breath, and what courage she could find, and joined him.

As she waited in the kitchen for him to return from stoking the fire, she felt no warmer than she had outside. She shoved off her hood and glanced around, marveling again at the equipment, the gadgets, the appliances. If her mother saw this she would think she'd died and gone to heaven. Heaven intruding once again on her thoughts pulled Livia up short, yanking her back to the situation at hand, twisting the knot in her stomach tighter.

"Why don't you go into the main room," Mark said, coming through the swinging door. He had shucked his jacket and wore a white dress shirt tucked inside faded jeans. He rolled the sleeves toward his elbows. "There's a fire going. I'll join you in a few minutes with coffee."

"Sounds good." The fire sounded especially good. Even her knee-high boots felt damp from standing in the downpour. She might have had stress-flu this past week, but she'd have the real thing if she didn't warm up soon.

"Go," Mark said, his gaze landing on her mouth, his eyes going dark. "Before your lips turn blue."

Before I have to kiss them warm, he seemed to be saying.

The moment shimmered with awareness and memory and Livia moved before it became an invitation. She hurried into the next room, the main salon where she'd been the night they'd chosen most of the dishes for the wedding, and on to the foyer. She hooked her wet coat on the hall tree, then glanced at her reflection in the mirror. She looked less like a drowned rat than she'd figured. She fluffed her short hair with her fingers, thumbed a smudge of mascara from beneath one eye. The tip of her nose was red and her cheeks were high with color.

Weather or nerves?

Probably both.

She smoothed her damp, calf-length skirt, straightened her sweater and went to the matching Victorian love seats that faced each other in front of the fireplace and settled on one, embracing the heat emanating from the burning logs. She could hear Mark in the kitchen, moving around, judged he'd be a while yet before joining her, and withdrew the copied articles from her purse.

The first thing to catch her attention was a black-and-white photograph of Ethan Marshall. He was a large man. *A chef. Like Mark.* Maybe that was the connection between them. Maybe that was how Mark had known Ethan. Maybe he'd worked with him. For him.

Though they shared the same profession, the men were opposites. Ethan had the girth of a man who not only cooked, but ate whatever he produced. Maybe even most of what he produced. He was as round as a pancake, as heavy as a deep-dish pie. But there was also an innocence about him. Something naive. Around the eyes. A look like the proverbial deer caught in headlights, a man in shock, wholly oblivious to the penalties he would pay for the crime he'd committed.

Oddly, she could not imagine the man pictured here killing anyone, let alone the mother of his son. But he had. They'd proven he had.

As she continued staring at the photo, a strange and deep sense of pity for Josh's father sifted through her. *God help such a man in the prison system.*

"What's that you're reading?"

Mark had crept up on her so quietly she started at his words. She breasted the pages and shook her head. "Nothing important. Something to do with the wedding."

This was not good. She was starting out their heart-to-heart with a lie. She hadn't meant to, had intended to use these articles as a conversation opener. She groaned at her cowardice, and felt a sheepish grin tugging at her mouth.

He placed the tray he carried on the coffee table. It held two mugs of coffee and a plate of pastries dripping with frosting. The aromas wafted into her, through her. Tantalizing, tempting, causing her mouth to water. Long ago, she'd trained herself not to give in to such urges, but since the day she'd sworn off sweets, she'd never felt the desire to indulge so strongly as she did at this moment—to just fill her mouth so full of sticky, gooey, cinnamon roll and frosting she couldn't speak.

He handed her a mug and only then did she realize it wasn't regular coffee. She lifted her gaze to his questioningly. The confidence left his face. "It's what you like, right? Latte with skim milk?"

He'd remembered after being with her once when she'd ordered it. She didn't think Reese, if asked, could name her favorite drink. But this man knew. Damn

Mark Everett. She didn't want to be touched by him physically or emotionally, yet she longed for the former and couldn't avoid the latter. Why did he have to know which coffee she liked? Photographic memory? Observant? Or had he made a point of knowing?

She clutched the papers tighter against her chest. "Why?"

"Why what?"

"Never mind." She shook her head. She wasn't going to ask about the latte. For all she knew, Bridget had told him her coffee preference. Besides, that was not why she was here. She lowered the papers to her lap, making no effort to hide them from him as he sank onto the seat across from her.

She said, "I lied. These are copies of newspaper articles about Wendy Marshall's murder and Ethan Marshall's subsequent arrest and trial."

He paled, his gaze falling to her lap, his hands curling around his mug, his mouth slipping into a hard straight line. He stared at the photograph of Ethan Marshall. "And what did you learn from those? That…that Ethan murdered Wendy?"

The defensiveness in his voice brought her head up with a jerk. "You don't think he did?"

"I *know* he didn't."

She recalled her own reaction to that photo. The innocent look in Ethan Marshall's eyes. She gazed at the picture again, then up at Mark, and felt a jolt of shock. His eyes were very like Ethan's. "You're related to Ethan Marshall, aren't you? A brother or cousin?"

Mark's expression went stony, unreadable. "Neither."

"Then what is your connection to him? Why do you

have a framed photograph of Josh's parents in your bedroom?''

He stared into his mug a long, tense moment, then lifted his head and pushed back a wayward lock of his ebony hair. ''Because I'm Josh's father.''

She set her latte down on the coffee table, trying to take this in. ''Are…are you saying you and Wendy Rayburn Marshall…had…were…lovers?''

He blew out a loud breath. ''I'm telling you that *I* am Ethan Marshall.''

Her mouth dropped open, and she glanced from the obese man in the news clippings to this flesh-and-blood one—whose body fat was nil—trying to reconcile the paper face with the one in front of her. ''No way. Except for a slight resemblance around the eyes…no way.''

''Yes, way.''

''Are you having some sort of delusion? Ethan Marshall is in prison for life.''

''I'm not delusional.'' He snorted. ''I was released a few months ago on a technicality.''

She shook her head. How was that possible? ''If…if that's true, why hasn't the state notified Reese's family?''

''For all I know, they have.''

''No. They think you're still in prison.''

''Really?'' He frowned at that. ''I know news coverage of my release was lost in the media feeding frenzy over the governor's sexual misconduct, but I figured the state would let them know, or some zealous reporter.''

Livia didn't understand it either. ''When were you released?''

He gave her the date.

"Ah," she said. "They were in Chicago for the basketball playoffs. Jay had gotten tickets and we all went."

"I didn't know, but I wasn't taking any chances of incurring further harassment from the Rayburns. I disappeared, had my name legally changed and re-emerged as Mark Everett. Even if the Rayburns should learn of my new identity, I doubt any of them would recognize me if we met face to face—since at the time of my release, the local news chain used an old photograph of me before I...I looked as I do now."

She glanced again at the black-and-white photograph of Ethan Marshall, then back at Mark. "How did you...?"

"Go from the Pillsbury Doughboy to Arnold Schwartzenegger?"

She blushed. "Yeah."

He smiled, but there was no warmth in it. "Prison isn't for wimps or ignoramuses. I was both. But I learned real quick that the Golden Rule—that crap we're raised on about treating others like we wish they'd treat us—is one hundred percent B.S. I'm no longer the gullible fool who trusted the law, who believed the truth would set him free."

"But your face is so...different." She understood the metamorphosis that occurred losing a great deal of weight. She'd lived it. But it hadn't altered her face the way it had his. "No longer recognizable...as Ethan's."

"No longer the pretty boy of my innocent youth." His laugh was biting, clipped, filled with self-derision. "Nose was broken twice. Jaw once. Doc put me back together as best he could, and I took care of the rest—by funneling my anger into exercise. Prison reshaped me physically and mentally. My enemies even began to respect me. Fear me. Avoid me.''

Livia cringed as her imagination ran wild at the horrors he'd suffered, things he'd described, things he hadn't, at the scars that showed, at the scars that didn't. She wanted to reach out and touch him, but feared he'd take it as pity and would resent her for that, think she was being condescending. But she did pity him. Did hate all that he'd been through.

All that awaited him.

Despite herself, she said, ''I'm sorry.''

But he didn't get angry. Instead he seemed surprised that she accepted his story at face value, and she realized he wasn't used to people taking him at his word. How difficult would that be to live with? Her heart ached for Mark. For Josh. Oh, God, the little boy's room upstairs. The unused toys, the empty dresser and closet. The dinosaur theme throughout this man's living quarters. Confusion settled over her. ''If you've been free all these months, why haven't you reclaimed Josh?''

''I can't.'' He put his head in his hands.

She struggled the urge to go to him, to gather him in an embrace. ''I don't understand. A court order or something?''

''No. My choice.''

She straightened. His choice? He chose not to reclaim his son? No. She didn't believe that. ''Then why were you following us that day in the park? Spying on us?''

He lifted his head and his eyes were so tortured she caught her breath. ''I can't stay away from him, but I must.''

''I don't understand. Why must you?''

Mark leaned toward her, his forearms on his thighs. "He was only three when he lost his mommy, then his daddy, every sense of security he'd ever known snatched away from him. Can you imagine how that felt? I can. And I'm not risking his going through it again."

"Why would he, now that you've been released?"

"I've been released on a technicality of the law, but I haven't been proven innocent. My son thinks his father killed his mother. The whole world thinks that. But it's not true." His gaze implored her to believe him, conveyed that it was important *she* believe him. "I didn't kill Wendy."

Livia *did* believe him. But then, she knew something no one else did. Cold-blooded murderers reserved an eternal spot in damnation. *This man* was slated for Heaven, not Hell. But if he hadn't murdered his wife, who had? "So, you want to prove your innocence before claiming your right to Josh?"

"Yes. I won't risk putting him through more torment. But it's hell. I see him so lonely—" his voice cracked "—and I almost give it up." His expression tightened. "But I can't. Not until I figure out who killed Wendy and why."

She let this sink in for a while and finally understood. "You need to get back into your wife's social circle in order to find her killer. Who do you think that is?"

"If I knew the answer to that..." He blew out another breath and finished off his coffee.

She took another sip of her latte. It was no longer warm. She drank it anyway, needing to cool the hot suspicions tripping through her. She set down her mug and peered at his ruggedly handsome face, her heartbeat escalating. "The reason you've insisted on catering my wedding to Reese Rayburn is that you believe someone in the house, in the family, is the real killer."

He sighed, but nodded. "Yeah, I do. It's the best bet."

Livia felt as though someone had settled an espresso machine on her chest. Not only was it possible that Reese or someone else in his family had killed his sister, but Josh, poor sweet lonely Josh, was going to lose his daddy all over again in eighteen days—maybe to his mommy's killer—if she and Mark didn't find the real killer before he or she shot that fatal bullet.

Her hand went to her mouth.

"I know this is a lot to digest." Mark stood and gathered their mugs. "I'll get some more coffee."

Livia nodded. She lurched off the love seat and went to the fireplace, added another log, then stared at the flames as they took hold.

Mark returned with a fresh latte for her and something strong-scented and black for himself.

As she sat opposite him again, Livia held the hot mug in both palms, the searing heat keeping her centered. "Tell me about her. About Wendy."

He grimaced.

"O-ka-a-y, that was way too insensitive." Oh, God, why had she asked him that? Obviously the memories were too painful. He'd loved Wendy. She reached to the plate of pastries, tore off a piece, then put it in her mouth. The delight of flavors, sticky dough, cinnamon and vanilla icing, meshed on her tongue, would go straight to her hips—fair punishment, she decided, for wounding this man she wanted to save not hurt. "You don't have to talk about her."

"Maybe I do. Maybe it would help me figure out why someone would kill her."

Livia grabbed the papers and shuffled through them until she came to a photograph of the dead woman. Wendy Rayburn Marshall had been lovely, elegant and thin in that way some people are naturally. *It must be nice.*

She reached for another piece of pastry, having to admit—as the savory flavors exploded on her tongue— that Sookie hadn't been kidding when she'd said Mark Everett made sinful pastries. These were absolutely sensuous. She licked her fingers, caught Mark watching, his eyes darkening. Her pulse shivered sweetly.

Mark cleared his throat. "I was going to culinary school when I met Wendy. I was surprised she'd have anything to do with me." He pointed to the photograph on her lap. "I mean, look at her. It's easy to see why I fell in love with her, but I never understood what she saw in me."

He gave a sarcastic laugh. "I thought maybe it was my cooking. I've never known a woman who could eat so much and not gain an ounce. I didn't know then that she was bulimic. I'd never heard of bingeing and purging. I didn't know then that she'd sought me out. Didn't know that in picking me, she'd chosen the least acceptable groom for a Rayburn bride that she could find, who still met her purposes and criteria."

"What criteria?"

He took a long swallow of coffee, then leaned forward onto his thighs again, coming closer, causing the air between them to feel charged, electric. She felt like a magnet being pulled toward its mate. "Wendy's college major was business, and when she faced graduation, she discovered that her father, Phillip, would not be making room for her at Rayburn Grocers. Her grandfather had set up the corporation to pass through the male family members, and if there were no male heirs the business was to be sold. Phillip concurred with his father. He said women belonged in pursuits other than running companies.

"Wendy was furious, but she had money of her own, left to her from her mother's estate. She decided if her father wouldn't let her work at the company business she would start her own business. A restaurant. But first she needed a chef. A man she could manipulate, someone who could cook cuisine that would make all of her wealthy friends steady patrons of her restaurant, someone her family would find totally repellent. I fit that criteria perfectly."

The hurt Livia had suffered overhearing her classmates joke about her eating her entire birthday cake clawed her heart with sharpened talons, the ache new again, fresh, not old, not dealt with. She knew exactly how Mark had felt discovering how the wife he adored actually found him repellant.

"I'm sure she…" But his don't-go-there look made Livia regret the attempt at empathy. How could she be "sure" of any motive Wendy Marshall might have had? She'd never met the woman. Knew her only through recollections contributed by Reese, and those were few and far between. As she thought of that now, she wondered why her soon-to-be-ex-fiancé seldom mentioned his half sister.

"It says in the papers that you discovered she was having an affair with someone and that's why…why… you…or whomever…"

"There was no affair. If anything, Wendy was asexual. She could take it or leave it." His features clenched as though he thought that might have been because of some inadequacies on his part.

The image of his naked, aroused body flashed into her mind, along with the other memory: the feel of him large and hard against her belly, the sheer sizzling need his kiss aroused. Granted, she hadn't known Ethan, hadn't kissed him, or seen him naked, but Mark had no cause to fear his sexual prowess was lacking in any area.

She considered telling him, but decided it might end up in a "prove it" battle of wills, and that was a war she could too easily lose. Or win. She blushed and clamped her lips tight.

Mark ran his hands through his hair. "I didn't kill her. I hardly saw her. I was readying Marshall's—our restaurant—for our grand opening. She was handling the business end, the books, the money. I was in charge of the kitchens, the menus, the food, the wines."

"What happened?"

"That's just it...I don't know. I wasn't there. I was at the restaurant."

She nodded, drank latte, then said, "What can I do to help you find out the truth?"

His eyebrows arched. "Why would you want to?"

"Because I have to."

"*Have to?* For Josh?"

She adored how his first thought was always for the boy. He gazed at her with something like awe. "You'd do this for my son? Maybe prove that your fiancé murdered his own stepsister?"

"Half sister."

"Stepsister," he corrected. "Reese was not Phillip's natural son. You didn't know that? Man, it's what really drove the knife into Wendy's heart. That her father would choose his adopted son over his natural daughter. She had something to prove.''

"So do we.'' She caught hold of the hourglass. "Not just for Josh—but for *us*.''

"For *us?*'' He looked unnerved. "Lady, there is no *us*. What happened the other day…that kiss…it was a mistake.'' His gaze landed on her lips like another kiss. His chest heaved, and he jolted to his feet, plunked the mugs and the plate of pastries onto the tray and strode to the kitchen.

Livia chased after him, pushing through the swinging door. She caught up with him at the sink and grasped his upper arm, pulling him around. "You're wrong. We have a connection… You've sensed it.''

He gazed at her hand, then into her eyes. That connection and a shuddering awareness—an awakening arousal—swept through her. The hourglass vibrated against her thundering heart. The air seemed filled with rapid breathing, charged with restrained need.

A muted bang sounded from somewhere outside, like a car backfiring, then glass exploded at their backs. Mark reacted with blinding speed, grabbing Livia and dragging her to the floor in a huddled crouch. "What the hell was that? Are you all right?''

She did a quick assessment. Nothing bleeding. Nothing broken. "I think so. You?''

"Yeah.'' He motioned for her to stay down, even as he raised up on his haunches and peered over the kitchen counter.

Livia knew she should heed his warning, but she had to see. Had to know if what she suspected was true. She eased up and spied a small round hole in the window above the sink. Her mouth dried, her palms went damp.

Mark shook his head, then, keeping below window level, he glanced at the wall opposite the sink as if trying to find something. "Looks like a damn bullet hole."

She shuddered and sank to the cold, tile floor, hugging her knees to her chest. "Oh, God, I was afraid of that."

She lifted her gaze to meet his, finding his eyes hot, fierce. He scowled. "What's that supposed to mean?"

Chapter Nine

MAKE MINE I SCREAM

One Scoop Fear
One Shot Fudge
Don't Forget the Nuts

"Where's your phone?" Livia's gaze careened around the kitchen, searching as she scrambled to her knees.

"Stay low!" Mark's hand landed on her shoulder, pressing her down so that she didn't raise above the level of the counter. He seemed less concerned about himself, cautiously scanning the backyard and beyond. "Damn."

"What?" Panic filled her stomach. "What is it?"

"Our shooter is getting away."

She leaped to her feet, but all she saw was a flash of taillights as Mark yanked open the door and tore outside into the rain. Livia heard a swerving fishtail squeal of tires on wet pavement, then Mark cursing. He stormed back inside and locked the door.

She was gripping the counter. "Did you recognize the car?"

He shook his head, water shedding from his hair.

"Didn't see enough of it. Might have been black, or navy, or any dark color."

"Then we don't know who." Growling in frustration, she started toward the other room. "I'm calling the police."

"No." Mark caught her by the upper arm. "No police."

"But we have to, Mark," she insisted. "Someone just shot at us and it wasn't with some BB gun."

His expression darkened, his voice hardening. "No police."

"But..."

"Let me tell you about the police." He leaned into her, his face inches from hers. She could smell the rain, feel it steaming off him. He said, "They'll come out here, look around, file a report and strongly suggest I stay away from undraped windows. There's nothing they can do. There's nothing they *want* to do. As far as they're concerned I'm a cold-blooded wife-killer who weasled through a loophole in the law. Their only regret will be that the bullet missed me."

She sucked in a breath, catching a whiff of vanilla tinged with cynicism and truth. She supposed if she'd experienced even a quarter of what he'd been through she'd feel the same distrust of the very agency that was supposed to protect the average citizen.

He said, "What have you done that led the killer to discover my identity?"

"What have I—?" Indignation flamed into Livia's cheeks. "What makes you think *I*—"

He leaned into her, his face inches from hers. She could smell the rain, feel it steaming off him.

She sputtered, "W—well, I admit I have been trying to gather information on Mark Everett. But honestly, it was only a clumsy attempt on the Internet and I didn't find out anything more than anyone else could.''

"Then how…?"

"How should I know?" She schooled herself to calm down. "Maybe someone recognized your voice. Maybe Sookie."

He glanced at the bullet holes in the window and wall. "I never imagined *she* was capable of firing anything more lethal than an insult, but I guess I shouldn't dismiss her out of hand just because she *appears* to have the intellectual depth of her nail polish."

Livia shivered. She'd known there would be a bullet to contend with this month, but she hadn't expected more than one, or that she'd need be concerned about being shot this soon. "Do you think he—or she—might come back?"

"I don't think he'll risk it. He's lost the element of surprise." His voice softened as his gaze steadied on her face, those golden eyes bringing to mind the bright light she'd seen leading into Heaven, but this light seemed the entrance into a heaven here on earth.

As though his look could cause the very earth to move, the hourglass quaked against her chest. She gathered a wobbly breath. "Surprise. Yes. It *was* rather surprising, wasn't it? Unexpected, even. What rocks have *you* overturned in your effort to prove your innocence, Mark?"

"Nothing." He straightened, stepping back from her. "Yet. I haven't had access to any place where I might find evidence."

"Then why the attack today?"

He shrugged. "You're the one who suggested someone knows Ethan Marshall is out of jail and calling himself Mark Everett."

"True, but—think about it, Mark—what threat are you to anyone at this point?"

He frowned and considered. "You've got me. The only thing I know for certain about Wendy's murder is that she was killed with my favorite carving knife in order to frame me."

Livia shoved the gruesome mental picture this formed from her mind and considered her own question for a long moment. "Are you sure you don't know something you don't know you know?"

He blinked, humor flickering in his eyes. "The surprising thing is, I actually understood that question, but the answer is no."

She found nothing in this situation the least humorous. Someone was trying to kill them and they didn't even know why. The hopelessness of their situation left her suddenly chilled, bloodless.

As though he, too, felt the chill, Mark nodded toward the swinging door. "Let's go back to the fire."

Moving into the other room was like stepping into another dimension. Here, the windows were draped. The privacy, the semi-darkness, the soft crackle of the fire wrapped around Livia, and she felt a much needed sense of security returning. False or otherwise, she embraced it, but she wasn't as steady as she'd been when Mark was holding her, wasn't as steady as she'd thought.

Hell, what *had* she thought? That it was possible to mentally prepare for confronting the person who'd shot her, who'd killed her, who meant to do it all again? How did anyone prepare for that?

Mark caught her as her knees began to buckle, his arm wrapped her waist, and he pulled her against his side. "Hey, hey."

"Oh, God, Mark, this is so awful. Worse than I even imagined."

"It's just shock, you'll be all right once it wears off."

This wasn't going to wear off. She had to tell him. Now.

Words, however, failed her as he helped her to the love seat, sat beside her, speaking in low, soothing tones, touching her hair, his fingertips feathering her temple. His gentleness moved her more than if he'd been bolder, rousing the need for him that she could barely contain.

She gazed up at him. He was staring at her lips with such a longing in his eyes that her blood began to heat. His face was centimeters from hers, his sweet breath as heady as an aged liqueur. As though he'd been privy to her thoughts, had read her mind, her heart, he said, "Lady, you are more dangerous to me than any bullet."

Oh, no, that was so wrong. "No, I—"

But he cut her off, his mouth taking possession of hers with a need so contagious she caught the fever on contact. Whatever weakness had befallen her knees moments before now swept her entire body. She dissolved against him, into him, her arms slipping around his neck, her tongue into his mouth. Damn, he tasted as good as he smelled, and kissing him was like nothing she'd ever known, as though someone had thrown her "on" switch, sending electrical current to all of her circuits.

Had she ever been more alive, more buzzed with energy, with untapped want? Every sensation seemed pronounced, vivid, every dancing twine of their tongues intoxicating. Her mind whirled, and her blood sang a melody sweet and pure and true. Her fingers slipped into his dense hair, played in its silken depths, and she realized she was memorizing the moment, searing it into her brain, storing it where she may need one day to go and pull it out.

To remember.

To relive.

To mourn.

Her fear of losing this man spread with a furious speed the fever to possess him. She was liquefying right here on his love seat, her bones gone to mush, her blood to scalding water, her will from steel to honey.

His hand found its way under her skirt, up her thigh, to the leg band of her panties, and she sighed his name, "Mark. Oh, Mark, please, make love to me."

If she'd dumped a bucket of ice on him, he couldn't have acted more startled. He jerked and pulled away from her, his hand sliding from beneath her skirt. He seemed to choke on his breath, his voice a raspy groan. "No. No. I can't do this."

He *couldn't* do this? Livia glanced at his fly, eyeing the huge bulge that contradicted his words. Whatever his problem, it was *not* physical. He was as aroused as she. "You want this as much as I do."

"No. I mean, yes, but no." His expression softened. "See, you don't really want this. You're in shock. Confused. Scared. Reaching out for solace. It's not every day you find yourself on the business end of a bullet."

How dare he tell her what she was feeling? What she wanted and didn't want? As though she were recalling the minutes before her death, Livia felt a burning in her chest, his words tearing through the soft tissue like so much shrapnel, ripping into her heart, her pride, her self-esteem—leaving her bleeding, humiliated and just plain furious. "You don't know what you're saying."

He stood with an effort and crossed to the fireplace,

put his arm on the mantel and stared into the flames. "You know, I actually thought I'd like nothing better than to bed Reese Rayburn's fiancée. I wanted to mess with his mind, to pay him back for all the crap he gave me while I was married to Wendy, for the hell he put me through when she was killed, to stick it to him for taking my child, then ignoring the boy. In theory that revenge greatly appealed to me. *In theory.*"

He blew out a noisy breath. "Damn it to hell, I didn't reckon on *you.* On caring about *you. For you.* I can't act on our…whatever the hell it is. I won't take advantage of *you* for the sake of vengeance against Reese."

He continued to stare into the fire, unable or unwilling to see the effect his confession had on her. He'd likely be surprised to discover that it had lessened the sting of his rejection, even endeared him to her. She studied the tense way he held himself and spoke softly. "I'm not going to marry Reese."

He jerked around, his gaze searching her face, zeroing in on her hand. "You're still wearing his ring."

"And I'm going to go on wearing it and go on acting as though I'll marry him on the twenty-eighth as scheduled, but it won't happen."

"Why not?"

"It's a long story." She went to stand beside Mark, reached up and touched his jaw. She wanted to tell him that he was the reason she couldn't marry Reese, wanted to run her hands greedily over him, wanted to start again what they hadn't finished. He didn't pull back, but he tensed as though ready to do just that— not, she understood now, because he wanted to, but because, despite every rotten card life had dealt him, he'd retained his basic principles.

She fisted her hands at her sides and forced herself

to set aside the desire racing in her veins. He deserved the same consideration he'd offered her, deserved to know that the person who'd shot at him today meant to kill him this month, deserved a chance to fight for survival.

Just as Josh deserved his daddy.

"Mark, about that long story…what I've been feeling isn't a reaction to shock. It's not going to wear off or go away."

"Yeah, I know," he said, moving back from her as though he didn't trust himself not to grab her again, to kiss her again. He stood behind the love seat, bracing himself against the frame. "But whatever your long story is, I hope it doesn't include me. I don't have anything to give to anyone at the moment. Not even my own son. I have no future until I've found Wendy's killer and proven my innocence."

She clutched her hands over her pounding heart. "Neither of us has a future unless that happens, and soon."

"Even when it does happen, don't expect any commitments from me. There's only enough room in my heart for my son."

"You don't believe in romantic love?"

"Been there, done that, have the T-shirt."

Great. She'd fallen for a man who'd sworn off love, who would soon be dead. Every emotion he denied feeling seemed to weigh her down, and Livia's chest ached. For him. For herself. "Mark, about my long story…I'm afraid it does include you."

His eyebrows lowered and he grew silent, still, his gaze pinning her. "Oh, yeah. And how is that?"

The heat of the fireplace stroked the back of her calves, making her too warm in her leather boots. She returned to the love seat and sat down.

"You aren't going to like it." A derisive laugh tripped from her. "Ha, what am I saying? You aren't even going to *believe* it."

"Not much surprises me these days. Try me."

Lord, how did she put this into words? She gathered a deep breath, licked her kiss-tender lips, and blurted, "One of us is living on borrowed time."

"One of *us?*" He straightened and flipped his hand at his chest, then at her. "*Us,* as in *me* and *you?*"

She nodded, watching his reaction, trying to decide how to tell him, what words would convince him.

"Lady, everybody's living by the grace of God. It's all borrowed time." He shook his head. "So, exactly what the hell are you talking about?"

The last thread of hope that this could be told with ease frayed away. Her hand found the hourglass beneath her sweater and she touched it for reassurance. "Please, let me just say this, then you can rant and rave and call me a fruitcake or nuts or whatever else you feel like, but please hear me out."

He crossed his arms on his chest. "I'm listening."

"Please, sit down."

He seemed disinclined, then relented and sat across from her, arms folded against his chest again as though to distance himself from her emotionally.

She gathered a bracing breath, exhaled slowly and began. "We are connected, Mark, but it's not in any way you could ever have imagined, nothing you've experienced in this world."

"Well, since I've never been to any other world—"

"But I have been." Livia swallowed over the knot in her throat. "Nine days ago, I died from a gunshot wound."

"What?" Mark gaped like a man just discovering he'd been captured by an escapee from a loony bin.

She pointed a finger at him. "You said you'd listen..."

"Okay." He seemed to be rethinking that promise, seemed to be mentally scrambling to find a way out of this, any way away from her. "Go on."

She was surprised by how dry her mouth was. "After I was shot and I...died, I went through total darkness until I came into a bright—"

"White light," he finished, sarcasm dripping off both words.

"Yes." She glowered and persevered. "That's where I encountered the Processor."

"The what?"

"The Processor. He processes souls into Heaven via his special computer."

Mark's mouth twitched as though he were biting the insides of his cheeks not to laugh. "And he didn't process you through because..."

"Because I'm not scheduled to die for sixty years yet."

"Well, that had to be a relief." The laugh he'd seemed to be fighting burst from him, followed by another and another. "I've never heard anything so funny."

"It's not funny." She fumed. "The Processor informed me that I had taken a bullet meant for...for someone else."

Still chuckling, he asked, "Did this Processor tell you who the hapless soul was?"

She resisted the urge to tell Mark that the Processor had called him the "hapless chef."

"In fact, he did," she said. "Right after he granted me the chance to relive this month in order to change the outcome."

"To change the outcome." He began sobering and

considered this a moment. "You mean, to make sure that you don't get shot again and the hapless soul who is supposed to die does?"

"That's it exactly."

"I see. And what happens if you can't change the outcome?"

"Then I will die again and will have to be processed into Heaven despite it not being my time."

His eyebrows danced and his eyes darkened. "You're serious, aren't you? You really believe this occurred."

"I understand your incredulity. I wouldn't believe this story, either, if I hadn't lived it." *If there wasn't a solid gold hourglass on an unbroken golden chain hanging around my neck.* "But you can't afford not to believe me."

His sigh rang with pity...for her. "Why in hell would anyone buy this fantasy of yours?"

To stop him from another fit of laughter, she kept her voice stony. "On February twenty-seventh, one of us is going to be shot to death. This time, it is *not* going to be me."

And I couldn't bear for it to be you.

She stammered, "A-and...and Josh needs *you.*"

"*Me? I'm* the 'hapless soul' who was supposed to be shot?" he roared and jumped to his feet. *"Me?"*

"'The hapless chef.' Yes."

His gaze was like a sword skewering her to the love seat. Red climbed his neck into his cheeks, and his voice held controlled fury. "If Wendy's killer really shot you nine days ago, prove it. Tell me who it is."

Livia winced. "I don't know. I don't remember anything about my first time through this month. Nothing."

Swearing, he spun away and paced the length of the room and back. He looked less disbelieving when he returned, finally taking her seriously, as seriously as the bullet hole in his kitchen window. "If this is supposed to come down on February twenty-seventh, why were we shot at today?"

Dear God, why had they been shot at today? She blanched as an upsetting possibility came to her. "My knowing that I was shot on the eve of my wedding has changed things. Altered events by...by—" *By my caring for you.* "By my realizing I can't marry Reese. Maybe that's sped up the time frame. Oh, God, maybe it means we have less time than I originally figured."

She plucked the hourglass from beneath her sweater to check. The shimmery "sand" within had fallen to seventeen. This day slipping away.

Mark came to the edge of the love seat. "What's that?"

She started to lift the chain over her head, got it as far as her ears and a hot charge, like touching an exposed wire, zapped her fingers. "Ouch."

She released the chain, and the hourglass fell innocently to the spot between her breasts as she blew on her fingers.

"What happened?" Mark sat beside her.

"It shocked me. Apparently, I can't take it off."

"Bull. I'll do it." He grasped the chain, got as far as her ears and dropped it as fast as she had, cursing. "What the hell is that?"

"It appeared on my neck the morning after I died and the Processor granted me the gift of reliving this month. Do you understand? I didn't put it on, it *appeared.*"

"It doesn't hurt you?"

"Sometimes it vibrates, tingles, and other times it warms."

Gingerly he lifted the hourglass and inspected it, the

span of gold lay shiny and pure against the rough tex-
ture of his battered hand. "I've never seen anything
like it. Not with all these demarcation lines. And what
is that inside? It's not sand."

She shrugged. "My best guess is stardust."

As fantastic as her suggestion was, he seemed less
given to dismissing the possibility out of hand as he
might have earlier. "If what you've told me is true,
then no matter what we do, one of us will die at the
end of the month."

"Maybe that will be the outcome, maybe we can't
change our fates, but we can try. I mean, it can't be
impossible. I've already changed something—my intention to marry Reese. I'm sure I hadn't done that
before meeting the Processor because I was adamant
that I was getting married the following morning."

He tilted his head to one side, the boyish gesture
charming, reminding her of Josh. "Wouldn't it be easier to disappear until March?"

"Survival by avoidance? I tried that. Remember the
day I fired you? You'd have none of it. You took to
following me, even going so far as to enlisting my
sister's help, until it seemed no matter what I did, by
trying to avoid the trouble, it was going to find me."

He offered no apology, just a sheepish grin that said
he'd do it again if need be.

She continued, "That's when I realized I could only
be in control if I confronted the danger head-on. I set
out to discover who you were and why someone
wanted to kill you. I figured knowledge would keep me
safe."

"Well, now you know all my secrets and you're still
in just as much danger."

"We both are and running away won't protect us."

He was still holding the hourglass, staring at it with

something between suspicion and disconcertion. She saw it move against his palm, saw his eyes widen. He lifted his gaze to hers and the heat she intuitively knew was warming his skin seemed to leap from the timepiece and into his eyes, awakening that eerie awareness that connected them on this plane and on that other, Heavenly one.

Several heartbeats clicked by, then Mark broke the silence. "Do you really think we can figure out who killed Wendy?"

"We have to. It's our only hope. And time, as you can see, is slipping away."

He released the hourglass, swallowed as it gently settled between her breasts, then dragged his gaze to her face. A nerve pulsed in his throat. "I'm not sure what we're looking for, whether or not there is anything to find, or even where to start a search. Are you?"

"Maybe some of the articles I copied—" Livia broke off, struck by a stunning realization. Her hand flew to her mouth. "Oh, my God, Mark. That's why we were shot at today. There *is* something to find."

Mark let out a whoop and grabbed her. She came into his embrace as though blown on an ethereal wind, moved by forces beyond her very will, her arms circling his neck, her mouth reaching up to meet his, and Livia felt as though she were being swept into an erotic tidal wave.

She slipped off Reese's ring. She wanted nothing between herself and Mark. For this passion, this man, all hers for such a short time could not, would not, be denied. Not this time. Not when making love with him, even this once, might have to last her an eternity.

Chapter Ten

S'MORES

Any Sweet Dessert
For Two
Indulge Until Sated
Then, Have S'More

"Livia," Mark moaned against her ear, her tender, delicate ear that was so soft and sweet he wanted to nibble it with his lips. He didn't want to hurt her, just take her into himself, make her part of him.

The need roaring through his veins ached for release, fast and furious, a quick sampling that he knew would only have him returning for more, much, much more. He'd been too long without a woman he was actually attracted to, one who roused fantasies, invaded his dreams, engaged his interest, made his blood hum, his nerves zing.

Hell, had he ever had a woman like that?

Like Livia?

Her hand furrowed between the buttons of his shirt, her soft fingertips grazing his stomach, loosening something deep in his chest, as though a layer of the armor that encased his heart had given way at her touch, as though she possessed the powers of the angels. Did she? Was that story she'd told him actually true? Had she—could she have been shot with a bullet meant for him, then been given another chance at life?

Just as he'd been given another chance?

But had he really?

Had he gained his freedom, been offered this hope of clearing himself, only to lose in a couple of weeks the future he prayed would be his and his son's? He gazed into her ardor-bright eyes and found his answer. The one thing he'd learned these past few years was that he couldn't control the future, he could only survive in the moment, and this moment was all Livia.

She began to unbutton his shirt and the sudden urge to live every second of whatever time he had in this skin entwined the need already coursing through him, making every breath, every sensation thrilling, exhilarating, intoxicating, cleansing from his mind all doubts, all concerns, anything that wasn't Livia; for despite his denials to her, his denials to himself, she was already in his heart, had already laid claim to him.

Making love with her would only intensify her hold on him.

Despite the danger of that, the fact of that, he could not resist the taste of her neck, her ears, her mouth, the feel of her yielding body beneath his exploring hands.

"Oh, Mark," Livia sighed as his shirt fell away, revealing the broad expanse of his chest. Buff bodies were her business, something she was used to seeing on a daily basis, but she'd never seen anything, anyone as beautiful as this man. Her memory of him naked had not done him justice. It wasn't that he'd sculpted his muscles to perfection, but that God had created him with a symmetry no man could gain by diet and exercise. His beauty was natural. Scars couldn't mar it, fat couldn't mar it, growing old couldn't mar it.

But would he grow old?

Would this chance to make love to him be her first *and* her last?

She laid her palm over his heart, felt it pounding beneath her fingers, the rhythm like the tap of a sexy dance step, quick, then quicker, mesmerizing, the beat vibrating into her, through her, heating the hourglass between her breasts, increasing the sense that this was the one man she'd been born to love, the one man with whom her fate entwined.

But were they destined to be star-crossed? One of them alive in this world, the other watching down from Heaven?

Mark's hand went under her sweater, across her stomach, her back, and every worry for what the future held dissolved in the heat of the moment, in the here and now, in the awareness that was Mark. Every breath seemed sweeter than pure oxygen, richer than gourmet chocolate, headier than aged whiskey, all tinged with the unique male scent and whiff of vanilla that was totally Mark. She sighed his name again.

His hands were lighting flames on her skin, searing her nerves, her flesh, melting her clothes into a puddle at their feet. She had expected she might be shy, but his golden gaze grazed her naked body with an awe that seemed to say she was more than he'd imagined, more than he deserved.

"Livia, you're so delicate, so lovely." Need rasped his voice and raised goose bumps to shiver across her skin. As bold as he'd been with her clothes between them, now he was tentative as he reached a hand toward her breasts, hesitating as if he hadn't the right, hadn't permission, as if once he crossed this line there would be no going back for either of them.

"Do it, Mark. Please." She caught his hand and brought it to her, leaning into his palm. The hourglass bumped against their joined hands and a flare of light radiated from within it, as glittery as a burst of stardust, as magical as the feel of his hand in hers. She kissed his lips, then his scarred hand, then brought his palm to her breasts, to her roused, sensitive nipples.

He closed his eyes, exhaling on a moan, then glanced at her as though he'd never touched a woman before, as though he were a virgin teen finally living his fantasies, eager with passion, timid with wonderment. Livia couldn't get enough of the soft abrasive slide of his skin against hers. Every nerve ending was swelling, growing more sensitive by the second, twisting desire into an exquisite coil in the core of her.

She released a joyous murmur and with it Mark seemed released from some self-imposed restraint, from whatever had been holding him back from taking what he wanted. His mouth dipped to possess her breast, and her pleasure leapt higher, deeper, flooding her with a new fire, this one liquid, molten, incandescent.

Mark's clothes joined hers on the floor and he eased her from the love seat to kneel upon them. He stood in front of her, fully aroused, more glorious than any man she'd ever seen, more glorious than he'd been last time she'd seen him disrobed, but this time she could touch him…and she did. The embers glowing red in the fireplace might be chips of ice compared to the heat emanating from his erection into her caressing hand.

She flicked her tongue against the tip of his arousal,

then kissed him, licked him, took him into her mouth. Mark tensed, and gripped her shoulders with an urgency that, between lovers, needed no words.

Livia eased onto her back and lifted her arms to him. He settled between her parted knees, leaned over her, took her head in his hands and lifted her face to his. As their lips collided in a fierce kiss, she felt his need probing the dampness at the center of her and could not endure another second's wait. She lifted as he plunged, and they came together with an explosive shock of sheer ecstasy that seemed to knock her world from its axis.

With every downward thrust, every near withdrawal, Livia felt as though she were spinning on a tornado of euphoria, lifted out of herself, rocketing with Mark toward the universe and into the stars beyond to burst through the Milky Way. Release came quick and hard, followed by myriad aftershocks, each one sweeter than the last, each leaving her breathless and clinging to Mark as he struggled to regain his own lost breath.

Livia was amazed that he made no move to disengage from her, as though he wanted their connection to last as much as she did. This was a new experience for her. In so many ways, she felt as if she'd never made love before, and she hadn't, not like this. Not with more than her body. Not with all her heart and soul.

She wanted to do it again, and again. Mark rose up on his elbows and peered at her with something like fear, as though he'd only dreamed she was here and couldn't quite believe this had actually happened. She lifted her hand and moved that wayward hank of hair from his forehead. "It was real, darling. It *is* real. As real as this hourglass."

"As real as you." He caressed her cheek, kissed her mouth.

She caught that whiff of vanilla again, and when he pulled back, she sighed. "God, you smell so...yummy...like vanilla."

He seemed surprised. "You can smell it?"

She felt him growing hard inside her again, and murmured, "Yes, always."

His eyebrows twitched and disconcertion flashed through his eyes, revealing for a brief second a private pain.

She whispered, "Tell me."

A nerve pulsed at his temple. "The only way I seem able to eradicate the stench of prison that is seared into my olfactory senses is by putting a drop of vanilla right above my upper lip."

He looked as though this might somehow lower him in her eyes, but though the mystery's solution was less romantic than she'd imagined, it only made her care about him more. "Well, I love it. It's the first thing I noticed about you, the first thing that attracted me to you."

A slow smile tugged at his sensuous mouth and she realized he was fully aroused inside her. He kissed the tip of her nose. "Thank you."

"For what?"

"For giving me a new perspective on my negative memories."

They shared a smile, then she moved her hips against his. "If you're really grateful...you could show me."

And he did...several times.

THE NEXT AFTERNOON Mark felt like a teenager who'd lost his virginity and couldn't wipe the grin from his face. He also had a new appreciation for sore muscles, though he ached in a good way. But in the cold light of day, without the bubble of rapture encasing him, he had to face and deal with the story Livia had told him.

It still seemed unreal, as though he'd been plunked into a sci-fi movie where all the players looked familiar but were actually cyborgs. He glanced at Livia, seated beside him in the catering van. She wore a pale blue turtleneck sweater and faded jeans beneath a sheepskin-lined denim jacket. Her frosted hair feathered her face, accentuating her aqua eyes, giving her an otherworldly, angelic glow.

Keeping him off balance.

Questioning his faith. His beliefs.

After the hell he'd been through, he'd no longer embraced the idea of Heaven, God, or an afterlife. Then he'd touched that hourglass Livia wore around her neck, and everything he thought he knew had been tested again. But how could he accept that this vital, vibrant woman had died and been given a chance to relive time that had already passed?

Was it any wonder he was disinclined to trust what his eyes showed him as truth?

The crinkle of paper called his attention to her hands and he struggled to ignore the memory of what those hands had done to him last night, and deep into the morning, what he'd like them to do again. She'd been quiet, thoughtful since getting into the van, fiddling with the edges of the food list they'd drawn up until the paper was dog-eared. She wore Reese's ring today, and he hated seeing it there even though it was necessary. They were headed to Rayburn Grocers to procure the items on the list for the wedding dinner, and he guessed she was mulling over what they were going to say and do once they arrived at the warehouse and began confronting suspects.

She surprised him by saying, "What we need to consider are motive, means and opportunity."

Mark braked for a red light. He didn't like this subject, but it was just as necessary as her wearing that ring. He fought to keep his voice even. "The means was a knife stolen from my restaurant kitchen."

"Yes." She tapped the now rolled shopping list against her palm. "Which is proof positive that Wendy's murder was totally planned with you as the intended scapegoat."

Her heart was in the right place, but her logic escaped him. "How does *my* knife being used to kill *my* wife prove *my* innocence?"

"It's obvious." Livia's voice brooked no argument. "It takes smarts to be a better-than-average chef, right?"

"Agreed."

"That's right. And no chef at the level of competency you've reached would commit a crime with his favorite, uh, utensil, then leave it behind for the police to find, still stuck in his victim."

It made sense. In fact, he and his lawyer had argued the same until they were hoarse; the police and the prosecutors hadn't wanted to hear it. "The thing is, apparently cops deal every day with criminally inept idiots who commit exactly that kind of stupid error."

"Yeah, well, maybe so, but the police don't know what we know. Nor, it seems, did they look further than their noses."

A horn blared behind them. Mark saw the light had turned green and eased off the brake. "The spouse is always the prime suspect when a wife or husband is murdered, and since the murder weapon belonged to me *and* had my fingerprints on it—as far as the cops and prosecutors were concerned it was open and shut.''

She sighed. ''Well, I guess I can't fault the police for employing a method that proves correct about ninety-five percent of the time.''

He felt no such generosity. ''Find yourself in that other five percentile group and see how magnanimous you feel then.'' He pressed the gas pedal hard, then hit the brakes. It wasn't raining today, but traffic was heavy and sluggish, his emotions as erratic as his reflexes.

Livia touched his arm, a reminder that he wasn't alone any longer, and his distress receded with an unexpected speed. In fact, the anger that seemed his constant companion these days had all but disappeared.

She said, ''I've been wondering if you can recall which of our suspects had access to your restaurant kitchen?''

He'd thought about *that* more nights than he could count—always with the same damned results. ''Probably all of them, I guess. Wendy thrived on showing off the place. She was especially proud of the kitchen. It was pretty high-tech.''

''Yes, but who'd been there *right before* you noticed the knife was missing?''

''I didn't know it was missing.'' He plowed his hand through his hair. ''It was there...in a set...but I hadn't used the knives. They'd been put through the dishwasher, then set out. If I hadn't checked those knives for sharpness, my fingerprints wouldn't even have been on them. And during that week, all the Rayburns were there at one time or other.''

Her face clouded, disappointment pulling her kissable lips into a thin line. "Then what about opportunity?"

He shrugged. "Since Wendy was killed at home, in the Rayburn mansion, our suspects all had opportunity."

"Damn. I was hoping we'd be able to eliminate someone, or at least narrow the field." She grew quiet a moment, then said, "That leaves motive. It's what I've said all along. If we knew *why* she was killed..."

"The police thought they knew why."

"The hell with their theories." She gave a dismissive snort. "We're after the truth."

Mark braked for another traffic light. Having Candee and Nanette believe in him enough to help get him out of jail had been wonderful, but having Livia believe wholeheartedly in his innocence, be as one hundred percent certain as he that he hadn't killed his wife, felt good in a whole new way. So did having the germ of hope that they might prove his innocence.

But that black cloud of possibly dying in the attempt to prove it hovered in a corner of his peripheral awareness. Out there. Dangerous. Imminent.

He glanced at Livia, his heart tripping. As much as he would fight for his life, for Josh's sake as well as his own, he would never allow this woman to take another bullet for him.

Her face was somber. "If it's going to bother you to discuss *how* Wendy died, I'll understand."

"No. It's okay. It was unbearable at first. Having to look at my son's mother in those gruesome police photographs in court, having to listen to her murder described in the most horrendous terms. But I've had three years to come to terms with the brutal facts. Some way or other, nature has insulated me from the pain of it and I can finally view it with the objectivity we'll need if we're to outwit her killer.''

She nodded. ''In those three years, you've had time to think about motive, Mark. Surely you've come up with one or two possibilities?''

''Not only have I thought about it, I've read up on the subject. Most murders are committed for jealousy or greed.''

''Love or money.''

''I could never understand the prosecutor's insistence that she was killed in a jealous rage,'' he said. ''Never mind that I had no reason to be jealous, the crime itself negates it. She was stabbed once in the back. That was cold-blooded. Calculated.''

''I agree,'' Livia said. ''The crime lacked passion. If jealousy and rage were behind it, she'd have been attacked with a viciousness that's missing. Probably from the front. And would have been stabbed more than once. Likely many times.''

''So, if not jealousy, that leaves greed.''

''Follow the money... Didn't you say Wendy had money of her own?''

''A small fortune, actually. She inherited it from her mother when she was just a baby, but the money was in a trust fund she couldn't touch until she turned twenty-six.''

''Which was the day before she died.'' Livia's eyes rounded. ''What happened to that money in the event she died before collecting it?''

''It was to go into another trust fund...for Josh.''

''Who's in control of that trust fund?''

''I was supposed to have been. It was in Wendy's will. She knew I'd never cheat Josh. But, of course, the law prohibits murderers from that kind of responsibility.''

''Then who is the new executor?''

''Reese, I assume. He wouldn't tell me.''

''And I didn't know to ask.'' She glanced up as he drove into the Rayburn Grocers lot and parked beside a red Jaguar. ''But I intend to find out. Today.''

Chapter Eleven

JELLIED ASPIC

Assorted Vegetables
A Couple of Tomatoes
Stir and See What Gels

"Well," Mark said, nodding toward Sookie's red sports car. "We wanted to confront as many as possible of our suspects at one time. Looks like something or someone is lending us an invisible hand."

"We have friends in very high places," Livia reminded him, glancing around the parking lot for the dark sedan that had sped away from Cupid's Catering shortly after the bullet had pierced the kitchen window, missing them by millimeters. But the vehicles were all on the lighter side of the spectrum.

She gripped the rolled page tighter in her hand, then realized she'd all but pulverized the food list Mark and she had drawn up. She uncurled it and began smoothing it over her thigh. The sensation recalled Mark's hands on this same thigh and the impulse to turn around and head back to his bed swept through her with the same urgency that prevented them from doing just that.

This morning when she'd awakened in her bed at her mother's, she'd discovered her worst fear come true—instead of being at the seventeenth mark, the stardust in the hourglass had slipped to fourteen.

By changing events, she'd altered something vital. Lost precious days, precious time. Time they could be together. Time to solve Wendy's murder. Livia's nerves were strung tighter than the tension bands of a rowing machine. *We have to unveil Wendy's killer and do it quickly. Or it's all over.*

"Ready?" Mark opened his door. He was looking at her questioningly, his golden eyes full of affection.

A shiver of desire darted through her. "Don't look at me like that."

"Like what?" The gleam in his gaze darkened.

Her breath knotted in her lungs. "Like you want to tumble right back into bed with me."

"Doesn't have to be a bed..." He started to reach for her, but she backed away, eyeing the front of the office.

He shrugged, but his look was still devilish, irresistible. "I can't help myself."

"You'd better manage," she said, struggling to take her own advice, to quell the sensuous, intimate tingles between her thighs. "The last thing we can afford is to be caught moony-eyeing each other."

"Do I make you feel moony-eyed?" He looked delighted at the prospect.

"You know you do." She grinned back at him. No man had ever made her feel as wonderful, as positively sinful, as Mark did. Even her mother had commented that she was glowing this morning. She prayed no one would guess the cause—because this glow seemed to come from deep inside and she could no more hide it than pretend she didn't frost her hair. "So, don't be offended if I ignore you in there."

She twisted the ring on her finger and wished she could take it off. She hated dishonesty, deceit, but she had no choice. Lives were at stake.

"Let's hope our attempt to rattle the guilty party works." He stepped out of the van.

Their plan was to show up as though they hadn't been shot at yesterday, as though no one in this building knew that Mark Everett was actually Ethan Marshall. They wanted to see who reacted. As plans went, it wasn't much of one, but since neither had a background in solving crimes, it was the best they could come up with. It wouldn't work, however, if she couldn't get her nerves settled, couldn't pull off the "happy, if somewhat harried, bride-to-be" act.

Mark asked, "You've got the list?"

"Here." She handed it to him as they walked up the steps and into the foyer. Mark had told her he intended to try to find a way they could get into the warehouse and offices tonight—after everyone else had left for the day.

A man, with his back to them, had his hip perched on the receptionist's desk, leaning down, talking to the buxom brunette. Ali threw back her head and laughed at something the man said, then she spotted them. Her laugh died. She looked guilty, as though she'd been caught flirting with someone's husband. Or fiancé.

Reese spun around. He looked as guilty as Ali, and Livia wondered whether the two were lovers, past or present. She didn't care—just found it interesting that she hadn't noticed before now, just as she hadn't realized why she was putting off planning her wedding. Reese's engagement ring no longer felt like a concrete block on her finger. No matter what happened in the end, she was lucky to have escaped marrying the wrong man.

"Babe," Reese said, glancing at Mark without curiosity as though he knew exactly who he was and what he was doing here. Had he seen the Cupid's Catering van? No, he hadn't realized they were there until Ali had. "Livia, I wasn't expecting to see you."

Obviously. She swallowed a grin. "You'll be relieved to know that I've finally decided on the menu for the reception."

"What I'm more relieved about is that you're over that nasty flu bug. I was afraid I might be stood up at the altar." Reese came to her and pecked her cheek like a chicken picking up corn in its beak, disregarding Mark. Dismissing him as someone not worth his consideration? As he would a servant? Or was Reese ignoring Mark on purpose?

Livia found a smile and motioned to Mark. "Our caterer is going to need to check out the food on our list. If someone can show him the warehouse."

"Of course." Reese extended a hand toward Mark. "Reese Rayburn."

"Mark Everett."

Livia could see the tension wafting off Mark, but Reese seemed oblivious to it. More concerned about himself than anything. Why hadn't she noticed that about him before? Had she not wanted to see it? Could a man that self-absorbed commit cold-blooded murder? His ego would probably give him to think he could get away with it. But what motive? Wendy's money? Was he now handling Josh's trust fund?

Ali was sucking her pinkie nail, her gaze crawling every inch of Mark, taking his measure. Livia couldn't discern, however, whether or not it was the healthy curiosity of a sensuous woman responding to a sexy male, or something else.

It hadn't occurred to her until now, but could Ali somehow be involved in this?

The more she considered the possibility, the more bizarre the idea that the receptionist had been the one who plotted the murder seemed. There could have been no love connection to Wendy—Ali definitely preferred men, though she wouldn't have given the old plump Ethan a second glance—and certainly no connection to Wendy's money.

"Ali," Reese said. "Would you please take our caterer to the warehouse manager? Hank Peterson will show you around, Mr. Everett. He knows where every pat of butter is kept."

Ali looked pleased to be of service. She rose with an erotic sway of hips and breasts—sure to lure any male animal with eyes in his head—and crooked a finger at Mark. Livia bit down a flash of jealousy and smiled at Reese.

He caught her by the elbow and pecked her cheek again. "Babe, come into my office and let's catch up."

She let him lead her into his lavish workspace. "I'd like to talk to you about Josh."

"Sure. He's been missing you."

"I miss him, too."

"We'll do dinner with him tonight, how about that?" Instead of using the sofa under the window where they could have been together, he went to his desk and sat down, gesturing her into the chair across from him as though she were a customer.

Livia's mind wandered to Mark—to *Ali* with Mark—and she had to force herself to concentrate on Reese. "Since we're going to be Josh's parents after our honeymoon, I think there are a few things we should discuss."

"No need to frown like that, babe." His smile reached into his stormy blue-gray eyes, but she felt the practiced charm beneath the grin. He'd gotten a haircut since she'd seen him last, his dark red hair cropped close to his head. *A man in control of his life and his woman.* "There's nothing we can't talk about."

Livia sat forward, her hands folded on her thighs. "I have some concerns."

"You shouldn't." Reese sounded as though he were selling her something. "You're great with the boy."

She knew exactly how good *she* was with "the boy." She loved the little guy. "Yes, but sometimes he seems so sad. As though he's still missing his mommy. I can't say I blame him."

"He was such a baby when she died, I'd have thought he'd be over it by now."

She felt as though he'd slapped her. She unsnapped her jacket with deliberate care, struggling to keep the indignation from her voice. "I'm not sure one ever gets over losing their mother. Certainly not to violence."

His expression tightened. "You think he needs counseling?"

"I think he needs parents who are involved with him."

Reese's face relaxed. "We'll be that."

She studied him as she said, "Tell me about Wendy."

The change of topic seemed to confuse him only for

the blink of an eye, then he shrugged. "Don't know what there is to tell."

"Last week, before I got sick, someone, I forget who, said she was your stepsister. I said half sister, but they said Phillip wasn't your biological father."

"I thought you knew." Shrugging, he made a face. "You shouldn't let it worry you. I'm a great endorsement for adoption. In fact, it proves we'll be great parents to Josh, even though he's not our biological son."

She tugged off her jacket. The room felt overly warm, but perhaps it was just nerves. "Did Wendy and you get along? Were you close?"

He seemed wound tighter than usual, like a beaker of kinetic energy. "You mean, close the way you and Bridget are?"

"Yes."

"Not really." He leaned back in his chair, and though she couldn't see it, she knew he was tapping one foot. "Wendy was a brain, a bookworm growing up. I spent my time as most boys do. Self-involved. Sports. The usual. But she knew so much about everything, I'll never understand why she hooked up with a fat slob like Ethan Marshall. The guy was a pig. Didn't take care of himself at all. Stupid, too. A buffoon. A real loser."

She winced at his callous attitude toward the overweight. Reese completely disregarded genetics and other factors. He thought all one had to do to stay thin was eat less and exercise. If only that were true. She'd lost weight that way, but if she didn't watch every morsel even now, even leading two or three aerobic classes a day, she would start gaining.

She asked, "Then you knew Ethan would kill her?"

"God, no." He stiffened, paling beneath his artificial

tan. "Who could have guessed that? I mean, he kept the violent side hidden from us all."

Did Mark have a violent side? She thought of his broken nose and jaw, his scarred hands. He'd certainly been shown violence, but had he initiated it? She would never believe that.

The *slap-slap* of feminine soles against backless pumps announced Sookie's approach. She was a vision in red, as usual, like a brand-new, wide-open tube of cherry lipstick.

"Livia, dear, hello. Ali said you were here. With that...*divine* caterer." She glanced at her son. "Jay is looking for you. He's in his office."

Reese's neck colored as if he hated being summoned like some flunky by his partner. "I'll be right back. Mother, why don't you tell Livia how the flowers are coming?"

Sookie *slap-slapped* over to the other customer chair and settled down. "You aren't worried about the flowers, are you, dear?"

"Not in the least. No one does flowers better than you."

"Why, thank you." Sookie pursed her carmine lips, as pleased as if she'd been handed a blue ribbon for a prize-winning rose. "So, tell me. Are *his pastries* as...sinfully wicked and delicious as Bitsy claims?"

Not nearly as sinfully wicked and delicious as the man. "I'm not much for pastries, but I have sampled his cinnamon rolls and they are to die for."

"Ah." Sookie sighed and closed her eyes as though savoring a taste she recalled, but that—given she was as dedicated to staying thin as Livia—she had probably, purposely not experienced since childhood.

Livia glanced toward the office door. Reese could

return any moment. "Sookie, I've been wondering lately about Wendy."

Sookie straightened as if Livia had poked her bony chest. "What a morbid turn of thought. Were you feverish with that flu, dear?"

"No." She fiddled with her engagement ring. "But since Reese and I are going to be raising her son, I think I should know something about *his* mother and who better to ask than *Wendy's mother.*"

"Wendy's *mother.*" Sookie laughed as though the word were a curse. "Wendy hardly considered me that. Wicked stepmother more likely. Nothing I said or did could penetrate that wall she'd built around herself. She was an unhappy child who grew into an even unhappier woman."

"Why was she unhappy as a child?"

Sookie waved a hand, sending her flowery scent in Livia's direction. "I'm no psychologist, but I'd say it was anger, pure and simple."

"Anger?"

"Well, of course. It's natural, isn't it? She lost her mother to the ravages of cancer at an impressionable age. Though Phillip didn't agree with me, I told him watching Anne waste away like that—Anne insisted on dying at home—had to have affected the child. It was obvious to me in how possessive she was of her daddy. For a while, she'd had him all to herself. Then I came on scene. In her eyes, I committed two major sins. First, I stole her daddy, then I tried taking her mother's place. With me in the picture, her daddy just never seemed to have time for her anymore. Plus I had a son, whom Phillip doted on."

Livia considered this a moment, then leaned toward Sookie. "Pardon me if this sounds insensitive, but I don't understand how Phillip could ignore his natural daughter and 'dote' on an adopted child.''

"Son," Sookie corrected. "I don't like to speak ill of the dead, but one of the things my Phillip found desirable about me was my son. He'd hoped we'd have one of our own, but it wasn't meant to be. So, he gave all his time and attention to Reese."

Pity for the sad and lonely and obviously unloved little girl who'd become Mark's wife and Josh's mother filled Livia's chest. There were worse things, she realized, than being raised in a home overcrowded with siblings, by parents who insisted on being involved in every aspect of your life. From this moment on, Livia vowed, she would never again complain about her childhood, but count it a blessing. "Poor Wendy."

"Save your pity, dear." Sookie crossed her thin legs and swung one foot, the high-heel pump dangling from her toes. "Wendy was a frustrated, manipulative witch. She particularly enjoyed exposing people's weaknesses or sensitivities to the ridicule of others."

Livia sat back, startled by Sookie's sudden lack of charity for her deceased stepdaughter. *So much for speaking ill of the dead.* It sounded as if she'd been the brunt of Wendy's ridicule. Had she? Perhaps Mark and she hadn't considered all possible motives. Perhaps someone, say Sookie, had permanently ended Wendy's tormenting ways? "Who is the executor of Josh's trust fund?"

Sookie looked taken aback by the question coming as Livia had meant it to—from left field. But before she could answer, Reese came bustling in.

"Oh, babe, dinner with the boy is off tonight. Jay just reminded me that we're taking clients to the Sonics game and—" he broke off, checking his wristwatch

"—I've just enough time to make a call. You and I'll do the kiddy-dinner-thing tomorrow, okay? Set it up with Joshie and get back to me."

"Right." Livia wanted to smack him for shooing them from his office, for relegating Josh to nothing more than an appointment on his busy calendar. Why did so many men always put business before family? Surely there were balances and compromises that one could make. She hated that Josh was every bit as lonely as his mother must have been. Mark and she were all he had. And if they didn't figure out who killed his mommy soon, he would only have *one* of them at the end of this. "I'll leave you a message after I've spoken with him."

Livia followed Sookie out into the foyer, catching up with her at the door. "About Josh's trust fund...?"

"How should I know, dear?" Sookie gave a dismissive wave of her long, sharp, glossy red nails. "I don't keep track of those things. Flowers and fashions, those are my passions."

With that she swept out to her car, as brilliant as a fiery sun moving toward the horizon, flaming the afternoon a fireball red.

"So," Ali said, startling Livia. She was leaning on the edge of her desk, long legs crossed at the ankles, short skirt hiked inches above her shapely knees. "Is that gorgeous hunk of a chef available? I didn't see a wedding ring or anything, but then some men don't wear them."

Livia twisted her engagement ring, totally understanding that some rings were only for show. "He's a widower."

"Recent?"

"No. A few years now."

Ali's dark eyes lit at that. "Steady girlfriend or anything?"

This was a complication Mark and Livia could ill afford. She decided to quell it before it got out of hand. She eyed the curvaceous brunette pointedly. "He prefers small blondes."

Ali's eyebrow arched as she returned the same pointed look. "And how do *you* know that?"

Heat climbed Livia's face. "He, uh, mentioned it."

"Oh?" Ali sucked on her pinkie nail, a little girl gesture. But there was nothing innocent in her big brown eyes, a look that conveyed she could change any man's taste in women given the opportunity.

Livia was not about to give her that option, not with Mark. "There *is* a woman in his life at the moment and from what he's said, it's pretty serious."

"Too bad." Ali sighed. "He's the most interesting thing I've seen in ages."

Jay-Ray strolled up to Ali's desk and dropped a file folder. "Five to ten you're talking about me."

The admiring glance Ali gave him was as good as an affirmation, but she added, "Who else?"

"Ah, I knew it," he said.

His grin was teasing, but Livia suspected he was serious. Jay-Ray lacked nothing in the ego department. He might be a model given his height, his short, bleached hair, his boyish good looks. Unlike Reese, who exuded a bottled energy, Jay-Ray was aged whiskey, smooth, slow, with a deceptive bite. He had a lazy gaze that made a woman feel important, attractive—including the lovely Ali who needed only to look in a mirror if she wanted confirmation of her beauty.

But he was, also, a man who paid attention to detail, who played the odds and often won.

Livia wondered if his love for gambling made him someone to connect to the money trail. Had he had access to Wendy's trust fund? To Josh's?

"Jay, who's executor of Josh's trust fund?" Livia blurted.

From the corner of her eye she saw Ali's mouth round. Jay-Ray started to speak, but Reese appeared, caught his arm and said, "Hey, let's get going. We'll miss the tip-off."

As though Livia hadn't spoken, the men strode past her, Reese slowing only long enough to peck the air near her cheek. Jay-Ray was rattling off the basketball stats of one of the Sonics' players to Reese as the door shut behind them.

Livia turned to Ali. "I don't suppose *you* know who the executor is to Josh's trust fund?"

"None of my business, sorry," Ali said, implying it was also none of hers.

Livia glanced out the window and saw that Reese and Jay had left in separate cars. She'd thought they were going together.

Ali said, "Looks like I can close up here and call it a day, too."

"I guess I'll go round up my caterer."

"I'm going to lock the front door, so you'll have to have Hank let you out through the warehouse."

"Sure." Livia went around the corner and into the hallway. She waited, pressed against a wall, her heart skipping too fast, her palms damp. The hum of the computers silenced, lights dimmed, then the front door closed and the sound of locks being engaged reached her.

Livia waited two full minutes, then crept back to the lobby and saw Ali driving away. Her departure sent a heavy quiet echoing through the offices. Livia slipped on her sheepskin-lined jacket, trying to stave off the creepy, shivery sensation that she needed to hurry.

She turned her attention to the receptionist's work area, to the row of cream-colored metal filing cabinets and found them locked. Each and every drawer. Where would Ali keep the keys? Frustrated, she spun to the desk. The computer monitor was dark, reflecting her own pale face back at her. She looked like the criminal she was.

No. Don't go there. Don't start feeling guilty about snooping. It might be dishonest, but it was necessary. Deadly necessary. She gripped the handle on the desk drawer. Locked. Damn, what did that woman do—take the keys home at night? Livia growled under her breath.

Outside she heard the rumble of an automobile. She dipped below the desk, peering over it. Cars paraded past in a mass exit, and she realized the warehouse crew was also leaving for the day. She blew out a breath. Mark and she would have the whole place to themselves, could pry at their leisure. Knowing he'd be with her at any second warmed Livia. She not only missed him, but could use his help.

She glanced at the computer again, her attention so focused on the task at hand, she failed to notice the dark sedan pulling past the front of the building and moving toward the warehouse.

But the driver saw her.

Chapter Twelve

PEEKING DUCK

Duck
Peek
Duck
Pique

In the low glow of the night lights, Livia stared at Ali's computer, wondering whether or not she could find something pertinent on it. She recalled Ali had said Josh's trust fund was none of her business—which probably meant there was nothing about it on this computer. Even if there was, could *she*—given her limited techno skills—find it?

Not likely.

Besides, what if activating the computer after hours set off a silent alarm or alerted Ali in some way? She thought about calling her brother Chad, the techno geek, then decided he was already asking too many questions about this whole thing. Had already caused the killer to know they were on the hunt to prove Ethan Marshall's innocence. She couldn't risk involving Chad further. But damn it all, why hadn't she paid more attention to the mini crash courses on the feeding and care of computers he kept shoving at her? That made her smile. Self-recriminations at this point were...well, pointless.

She glanced at her watch. What was keeping Mark?

She headed into the hallway again, deciding to try a search of Reese's desk and files. But his office door was closed. Locked. As was Jay-Ray's. Frustration filled her belly and tightened a band around her head. This was ridiculous. How had she thought she'd be able to snoop into anything private here? She should have figured out a way instead to steal keys from the suspects.

She'd better go round up Mark.

She followed the hall to the end and shoved through the double doors into the warehouse. The ceiling was two stories high with row upon row of twelve-feet-high shelves stacked with food, everything from dried apricots to canned zucchini. It was even more eerily quiet than the office area, darker, too. "Mark?"

He didn't answer and she called louder, then listened. Nothing but the low hum of the cooling system used for the refrigerators and giant freezer. Still, her own voice seemed to echo hollowly off the racks of food and the slap of her shoes seemed clamorous against the concrete floor.

She yelled, "Mark!"

No answer. Her muscles tensed. Something like the scrape of a heavy cardboard box being moved reached her from the end of the building. He was here, he just couldn't hear her. She hurried toward the sound, vaguely aware that the hourglass was warming between her breasts. "Mark, where are you?"

Although she'd shouted again, he still didn't answer.

Had something happened to him? The thought sent her heart racing. She chided herself to stay calm, not to jump to conclusions. If he wasn't in the warehouse, he was out in the van waiting for her.

But she didn't believe that for a second. He wouldn't leave her in here alone. So where was he?

With caution, she moved near the giant walk-in freezer. A large metal ice chest was propped against the open door, bright light and frosted air spilling out. ''Mark, are you in there?''

The hourglass grew so hot it felt like a match held to her chest. Warning her. Mark. Her mouth dried. Oh, God, something had happened to Mark. She knew it. Felt it. Suddenly felt danger all around her. She stopped and glanced around for a weapon. An open box of half-gallon juice cans stood on a shelf near her head. She grabbed one. It was huge and heavy in her small hands, but she was strong and could hit a target dead-center with a rock. This was bigger than any rock she'd ever thrown, but she figured she'd hit whomever threatened her.

Unless that person had a gun.

She crept to the freezer, took a deep breath and stepped into the opening, nerves taut, can readied, expecting anything. The cold air swept over her, and the sudden shift from near-dark to floodlight-brightness blinded Livia as if someone had snapped a camera flash in her eyes. ''Mark?''

As her focus returned, the hourglass vibrated, and Livia tightened her grip on the can. She moved carefully into the freezer. It was deep and wide and lined with shelves of frozen, boxed foods, alphabetically categorized. She stole down the first aisle and into the second, numb to the chill, heated by the fear searing along her flesh like flames on an oil slick.

She cleared the second aisle and started into the third, then stopped short of tripping over a frozen leg of lamb, its plastic covering drenched in something as red and thick as ketchup. She bent and touched a finger to the red goo. It smelled salty, acridly tinny. Blood.

Her pulse beat in her throat. She rushed into the next aisle and gasped, "Mark!"

The can dropped from her grip at the sight of him sprawled on the gelid concrete, his hair wet at the crown of his head, blood pooled on the floor. She rushed to him. Oh, God, was he dead? His lips. They were blue. "No, no, please."

She touched his neck, found a pulse, and released a heavy breath. Thank God, he was alive. But the wound on his head looked deep. She touched the area near it and realized the blood was sticky, tacky. She doubted it had congealed though, just stopped because of the below-freezing temperature in here. The cold had likely saved him from bleeding to death. "Mark? Mark?"

He didn't respond. She had to get help. She took off her coat and spread it over him. "I'll be right back, darling."

She darted for the door. But as she reached it, it slammed, inches short of smacking her nose. Livia screamed and stumbled back. Her chest heaved, the cold air burning into her lungs. She tasted her own fear, felt her knees go weak with terror. Wendy's murderer was on the other side of the door, had locked them in here to freeze to death.

No. Shot to death. That was how one of them would die. Not like this. Not locked in a freezer. Not both of them together. She inhaled several deep breaths, finally calming. Only then did it strike her that she'd changed the allotted time by falling in love with Mark. What else might that have changed? The mode of death?

No. She couldn't, wouldn't, let Mark die. She had to get him to a hospital. From somewhere deep in herself she found a courage she didn't know she had, and forced her rubbery legs to move. She grabbed the door handle. Locked.

For a split second she felt relieved at not having to face the killer. But the sensation fled. She had no idea how quickly it would occur, but she knew if they didn't get out of here and soon, they would succumb to hypothermia. She hugged herself against the waves of cold already penetrating her thin sweater and tried to think.

A groan from within the freezer brought her spinning around. Mark. She ran to him. He moaned again and his eyes cracked open. She knelt and touched his face. "Careful there. You took quite a slam to the noggin."

"What?" He started to roll onto his back, a hand groping for his head. His face was scrunched in pain.

"Someone whacked you on the head with a frozen leg of lamb."

"Hurts like hell."

"I'm afraid it split your scalp open. I have to take you to an emergency room. I think you need stitches."

"No hospitals."

"A doctor then. You might have a concussion."

"No. No doctors. Just get me someplace warm." He tried to sit up, seemed to reel and she caught his arm.

"I wish I could. But whoever struck you has locked us in here."

He frowned as though trying to grasp what she'd

said. Then he shook his head and winced. "No. That's not right."

"It's not?" She helped him to a sitting position. "Believe me, we *are* locked in. By the time help arrives we'll be matching Popsicles."

"No. A safety override." He grunted, shook off her jacket and attempted to stand. He got as far as his knees and swayed back and forth a moment, then stood with her help. "Come on. I'll show you."

He staggered through the aisles. Livia snatched up her jacket and put it on, following right behind him, ready to grab him if she had to. He stopped at the door, eyeing the area around its frame. He spoke haltingly, "Nowadays…freezers come equipped…with safety releases…"

"In case someone is unlucky enough to find themselves in our situation?"

"Exactly."

"You mean, we can open the door from *inside?*" Hope mixed with terror. What if the killer was still out there? In the warehouse? Waiting for them?

"The lever should be…ah, here it is." He gave the pull latch a tug, tilting over with the exertion. The lock release clicked and the door gave, darkness bordering the edges, but not swinging wide as it should have. Mark eyed it with leeriness, putting himself between Livia and the gap.

She caught his arm. "Mark, don't. The killer might still be here."

"Maybe so, but we can't stay in this icebox any longer." He was shivering; so was she. But Livia wasn't sure it was the cold causing her chills. Mark put his shoulder to the door and it moved another quarter inch, accompanied by a scraping sound. "Something's lodged against it."

"The ice chest, probably." She added her strength to his. The door inched wider. One more shove and they had it open enough to squeeze through.

"Stay here," Mark whispered. "Until I'm sure it's safe."

Her heart banged against her ribs. No way was she staying behind, leaving him to face whoever waited on the other side of the door. He began easing gingerly through the opening. Livia followed as though they were connected at the sleeve and pant leg, matching his every sideways step. Wisely, Mark didn't try to stop her.

Going from bright light to near darkness had her blinking and disoriented again. She wondered where the main switch was. She wanted to flood the warehouse with light, drive out the shadows, expose anyone hiding in the murk.

She cleared the door, and Mark grasped her wrist, yanking her down. She banged her shin against the ice chest and swallowed a cry of pain. She'd no sooner squatted when the crack of a fired gun resounded in the warehouse. The dim light at the farthest corner blew apart. Terror stabbed Livia.

The next bullet hit the light above them. Glass exploded and rained down on them. She flattened herself on the floor, hands shielding her face. "Oh my God, oh my God, oh my God."

"Shh," Mark admonished in a whisper. "Any noise makes our whereabouts easy to pinpoint."

The next bullet kissed the air above Livia, puncturing a sack of flour and powdering her shoulders. It dawned on her that with the light from the freezer at their backs, they were sitting ducks. She scrambled up and shoved the freezer door closed. Their little corner of the warehouse went black. She felt her way back to Mark, and whispered, "We need to reach the back door. It's our best chance of escape. This way."

Luckily, Livia had been in the warehouse many times and was familiar with the layout. The freezer abutted the end wall. The end wall held the exit door. With her back to the freezer face, she kept one hand on its cool surface, the other on Mark. For all the fear racing through her veins, the worst was the fear of losing him in the darkness, losing him to a fatal bullet.

Another gun burst shattered the last remaining light, pitching them into complete darkness. Livia sucked in a sharp breath and stopped. Mark bumped into her.

"Keep moving." His voice brushed her ear.

She nodded, forgetting in her fright that he couldn't see her. She could hear footsteps from across the warehouse. Whoever was in here seemed able to traverse the aisles despite the total darkness. Then she saw it. A beam of illumination poking through the shelves of foodstuffs. The shooter had a flashlight. Livia wanted to cower in terror, stop right where she was and curl into a ball, but Mark pushed against her, making her move.

Her shoulder bumped something solid. The end wall. She exhaled in relief and murmured, "We're here."

The bobbing light was coming closer. The hourglass warmed against Livia's skin, warning her. Fear filled her throat. She felt a scream building and struggled to rein it in. Suddenly the footfalls grew louder, faster. She knew then that the killer had spotted them, was coming to kill them, knew if she pulled out the hourglass to check she would see the heavenly sand had fallen to zero.

But the light played over the exit door, then went out. Livia's grip on Mark's arm tightened, her every muscle clenched. She couldn't see beyond her nose. She held her breath. The quiet was broken by the sound of the exit door opening, then slamming shut.

Mark swore and jumped up, dragging her with him. "He's getting away. Come on."

He moved out of her reach and in the darkness she stumbled after him, arms flung out, feeling her way. Mark seemed to have no problem figuring out exactly where he was. She felt lost in a fog, unable to identity basic landmarks.

"Livia?" He was at the door, yanking it open. The outside light fell across his outline.

She felt as though someone had torn a veil from her eyes. She ran to him. They raced out and onto the employee parking lot. It was empty. As they rounded the building to the office parking area, they heard the squeal of tires and spied a dark sedan darting into the thick traffic on the main road.

"Get in the van!" Mark shouted. "That snake is *not* getting away this time!"

Chapter Thirteen

CANDIED KISSES

2 Cups of Sugar
1 Pound of Chocolate
Heat to Bubbling
Makes It All Feel Better
For a Little While

Livia chased after Mark. He'd been knocked unconscious with a frozen leg of lamb, but sprinted with the speed of someone trained for a marathon. Adrenaline, she supposed. Hers had been stripped away, along with her stamina, by the fear coursing through her veins.

She arrived at the passenger side of the van out of breath, her heart pumping triple time. Mark already had the engine running. As she hit the seat and slammed the door, he smacked his foot to the gas pedal. The van shot forward and a second later plunged into traffic. Horns blared and tires screeched.

Livia braced for a crash, frantically snapping on her seat belt. They'd survived the freezer, survived being shot at, only to die in a road accident?

"Mark, slow down. Please. The light ahead is red."

He didn't seem to hear. Didn't seem to notice the glare of taillights as drivers braked for the traffic signal. The van careened from lane to lane, closing in on the bunched pack of idling vehicles. She scanned the cars at the stoplight, but there were too many dark sedans to figure out which one they sought.

The light turned green. Cars began moving, some going left, some right, some straight.

"Mark, please, slow down. This is impossible. Even if we could make this light—which we can't—which car would you follow? This is crazy. Senseless. We aren't going to catch him."

"I know, I know." He swore, tapped the brake and gave his head a furious shake, then grabbed it. "Oh, damn, oh, damn. I shouldn't have done that."

His hand came away bloody. He looked at his fingers as though he had no idea what he was seeing.

Her stomach clenched with new fear. "You're bleeding again."

He was pale, too, she realized, and strove to keep the fear from her voice. But she'd almost lost him. Could maybe lose him yet. "If you won't go to an emergency room, please, let's go to your house and tend to that wound before you bleed to death."

"Okay." He pulled to the side of the road. "But you'd better drive. I'm starting to see double and as delightful as looking at two of you is, one of you, Ms. Kingston, is more than this guy deserves."

Livia would argue him to the mat over what he deserved, but arguing with him was a waste of breath. she felt sure Mark had a concussion, but nothing she said convinced him to see a doctor. In the end she gave up, figuring the only remaining option was to cleanse and bandage his wound as best she could and pump some aspirin into him.

By the time they reached Cupid's Catering, Candee and Nanette had gone for the day. Livia studied the surrounding alley and backyard, praying the killer hadn't beaten them there, wasn't hiding in the darkness, somewhere out of sight, with a gun aimed at them. The possibility had her moving quickly, but Mark was less surefooted than he'd been only a short time ago. Leaning on her, he staggered up the back steps and into the house like a drunk, increasing her fear that his wound was worse than she knew.

She could lose him at any moment. Desperation to cling to him, to be with him, tore through her. Why had she never realized before that life was so precious? So short? That every minute should be cherished? Spent with someone you loved.

They'd been lucky…tonight. Been given more time to be together. She thanked God for these priceless gifts of time and love, and promised not to waste either.

Mark set the locks the moment they were inside.

She helped him upstairs to his private suite, into the bathroom, onto the closed toilet lid. She dug through his medicine cabinet and took out gauze pads, tape, antiseptic and disinfectant. She laid the supplies on the toilet tank, along with Reese's ring, which she would not wear while making love to Mark, then glanced at her patient.

His pupils seemed equal in size to her. But was that the only way to judge a concussion?

Despite the discomfort he had to be feeling, he grinned at her with a devilish glint in his golden eyes, and she knew he too was grateful to still be among the living, to have this time together. "Are we going to play doctor?"

"You wish." She grabbed a towel and the Mercurochrome, then positioned herself between his thighs and tipped his head toward her. "This isn't going to be nearly as much fun."

"See, there's the difference between men and women," Mark drawled. "From my perspective, as long as you're standing between my legs, I'm having a good time."

"You might want to reserve judgment on that." She dribbled stinging disinfectant into his open wound, using the towel to dab the spillage.

Mark grunted in pain. "Oh, yeah, we're having fun now. Yee-ha!"

Livia winced. She hated inflicting pain on this man she wanted to do anything to but hurt. She cleansed the wound, wiping away the congealed blood from his hair and scalp. To her utter relief, the wound wasn't as deep as she'd thought and she told him so.

"That's good news, nurse." His hands were on her thighs, moving upward, probably distracting himself from the pain, definitely distracting her.

Livia grinned. "You're a very naughty patient."

His palms cupped her bottom. "You ain't seen nothin' yet, nurse."

She felt her knees grow wobbly and strove to contain the desire that responded with wild abandon to his voice, his gaze, his touch. "I'm not a nurse, but growing up in a home with seven brothers and sisters I've learned basic first aid for everything from scrapes and scratches to gashes and gouges. So, hold still, you."

He obeyed, stilling his hands on her bottom as though he needed to touch her, to assure himself she was real, alive, not gunned down in the warehouse. When she was satisfied the cut was as clean as she could get it, she slathered on a layer of antiseptic, covered it with a gauze pad, then secured the pad with tape.

"Do I get a lollipop?" His gaze shone with need, telling her that she was the "candy" he wanted.

A responding shiver echoed through Livia. "How about some aspirin, instead?"

She handed him the pills and a paper cup of water.

He said, "Okay, I'll take the painkillers, but only if you'll kiss me afterward and make me feel all better."

Laughing, she took his head gently in both hands and kissed him near his bandage. "Is that better?"

"Not really. Maybe here would help." He pointed to his forehead.

She kissed him there. "Better?"

"A little. But I think this hurts, too." He pointed to his cheek.

She kissed him there, drinking in his wonderful vanilla scent. "How's that?"

"Almost, but not quite. How about…?" He lifted his face and pointed to his mouth.

Smiling at his antics, she leaned lower and his arms snaked around her, his lips meeting hers with such hunger she wobbled and dropped onto his lap. He tasted her mouth as no man ever had, first the upper lip, then the lower, then his tongue twined with hers and she became dizzy with the power of his persuasion.

Several sumptuous seconds passed before she recalled he might have a concussion, and she broke off the kiss, murmuring, "You should be in bed."

He reached for her mouth again. "I'd like nothing better than to lie down with you."

Desire seemed to be stealing the air from the room, leaving her panting, breathless, frantic to rip the clothes from them both and to end this erotic torture. But one of them had to be practical, levelheaded, had to look after his health. "I'm not sure this is the best thing for you...given your condition."

He brought her hand to the bulge between his legs. "I think it's the perfect prescription, nurse, given my 'condition.'"

All resistance left her. She stood, pulling him to his feet. She hadn't checked the hourglass but she knew when she did the sand would have fallen lower. They were running out of time, she felt it as surely as she felt the draw of this man. And she wanted to be with him, had to be with him, had to make love with him one more time. "Come on, you naughty patient. I'm going to treat you to my best bedside manner."

"I like the sound of that." His voice had gone husky, his gaze lusty.

She led him into his bedroom. Mark kissed her neck, one side then the other as she unbuttoned his shirt, as he tugged off her sweater and bra. Touching his naked chest, his flat stomach, the muscles on his broad back felt even more delicious than the first time and thrilling quivers scurried through her.

"I love this spot." Mark dipped his mouth to nuzzle the hollow of her throat. "Almost as much as this spot." He spread kisses along her collarbone to the edge of her shoulders. "But this might be my favorite spot of all." He nibbled his way to her breasts and his tongue stroked one supersensitive nipple, then the other, zinging heart-melting sparks through every part of her.

She caught the waist of his jeans as he caught hers,

his mouth claiming hers again, the eagerness wild, uncontrollable, and their clothes seemed to fall away on their own. Then she was holding him, tasting him, kissing him. She gazed up, meeting his look. He was swaying on his feet. She rose, kissing her way to his chest, urging him onto the bed, onto his back. He lay propped against the pillows fully aroused, as inviting a man as ever a woman could want, and she wanted him bad. She climbed onto the bed, straddling him.

"Maybe this is my favorite," Mark rasped. She lowered her hips to his, and he gasped as she sank onto him, taking him into her, deep, then deeper still. "Ah, yes, this *is* my favorite."

"Mine, too," she said on a quavery sigh. "Mine, too."

The hourglass heated between her breasts, growing as hot as Livia, arcing out that strange and eerie glow that seemed to enfold them, and she felt herself going liquid, like dissolving sugar, bubbling, sweet, fluid, crystallizing into one with Mark.

Ecstasy filled his eyes as she lifted her hips and brought them down, again and again, intoxicating her, spinning her body and soul high, then higher into a dizzying spiral that reached right into the clouds, halfway to Heaven. She burst through and into a transparent expanse somewhere between this world and the next, a place that only Mark could take her. She cried his name, gripped his hips, her head thrown back in abandon, her voice meeting his on that ethereal plane.

She collapsed on him and felt her heart thundering against his. Her breath was ragged, her body shivery with aftershocks. "I was wrong... That last is my favorite."

"Oh, yeah, mine, too." His breath was as labored

as hers, and she smiled at the luscious way she felt, as though Mark's lovemaking had released her somehow from every restraint she'd known in her life. She rolled to his side and he enfolded her in his arms.

They slept, wrapped together for hours. Livia woke ravenous. It was two in the morning. She left Mark sleeping and stole to the kitchen. She found chocolate sauce and strawberries in the refrigerator along with a bottle of sparkling cider. She heated the chocolate in the microwave, then set it all on a tray, along with goblets and napkins.

The strawberries were huge, more than a bite. She spied a hefty butcher-block knife holder on the counter near the stove. Each knife handle was forged metal engraved with a small cupid. One of the larger knives was missing. Probably in the dishwasher, she mused, grabbing a smaller one and putting it on the tray.

When she reached the bedroom, Mark was rousing. "What you got there?"

She smiled. "Sweet sustenance."

She joined him on the bed, settling the tray between them. He poured the cider as she sliced two of the larger strawberries, dipped them into the warmed chocolate and fed them to him. He was smiling now. "Yummy."

He kissed her, took a sip of cider, then fed strawberries drenched in chocolate to her, and not once did Livia think of calories. They made love again, put the chocolate and cider to even more erotic uses, then showered together. Afterward, Mark sat beside her on the bed as she dressed to leave, cajoling her to stay.

She shook her head. "I don't want my parents wondering where I spent the night."

"Oh, all right." Mark caught hold of the hourglass and alarm filled his eyes. "Look."

The stardust had slipped to ten. Livia's nerves jumped. As much as she wanted to stay with Mark, here in his bed until all of the time had passed, she knew they couldn't.

"There's no telling how much time we have left. The sand is slipping through this hourglass with no rhyme or reason." Mark swore. "We have to figure out who murdered Wendy."

She forced herself to shake off the fear and to concentrate. "Did you learn anything from the crew in the warehouse?"

"The biggest thing I got for my trouble was this lump on the head. Most of the warehouse workers are new since my time. Those jobs don't pay all that well and the turnover is huge."

Disappointment tripped through Livia. "What about the warehouse manager, Hank?"

"Closemouthed, loyal to the Rayburns. He looked at me funny when I asked about Wendy. So, I let it go. How did you fare?"

"No better than you, I'm afraid. After everyone left, I discovered the offices were locked as well as all the file cabinets."

"You didn't get anything from questioning our suspects?"

"Depends on how you define 'anything.' I still don't know who the executor is of Josh's trust fund. But I could probably assign motive of one kind or another to all of them." She told him what Sookie had said about his deceased wife, asking whether or not the accusations were true.

"As much as I'd like to deny it, Wendy did seem

to get some perverse pleasure from ferreting out people's secrets, then exposing them to an audience that would most embarrass her target.''

The way he said it made her wonder. ''Were you ever her target, Mark?''

''Yes.'' He grimaced. ''I thought she married me because she loved me. I didn't understand it, mind you. I just decided not to look a gift horse in the mouth. I was thrilled that she chose me. I mean, back then, she was *my* fantasy come true.''

He looked chagrined.

Livia touched his cheek. ''She was lucky to have you.''

''Maybe if I'd been built...more like I am now, she'd have felt the same.''

Livia wanted to smack something. She clamped her teeth, furious at Wendy for hurting Mark, for being so narrow-minded. ''True love has nothing to do with how heavy or thin someone is, with how pretty or handsome, either. True love is all about the spirit and the soul, Mark.''

''You seem pretty sure of that.''

''I am...now.'' She felt her cheeks heat. ''You know, that saying, 'It's as easy to love a rich man as a poor one, so marry a rich one'?''

He frowned, obviously not making the connection between one thing and the other. ''I've heard it.''

''Well, I believed it. Made it my mantra. As callous as that sounds now, it's what drew me to Reese. It's almost funny that I had to die before I could learn true love isn't calculating. Love comes from the heart, not the pocketbook.''

He touched her cheek and his eyes seemed to embrace her with the very emotion they were discussing. "And...it comes when you least expect it."

She cleared her throat. "I know."

"Livia, if I should die when the sand runs to the bottom of that hourglass—"

"No." She put her hand over his mouth. "We can't let that happen."

He pulled her hand away, kissed her palm. "But in case we can't prevent it, I want you to know that I'll always be grateful for this, for our time together, for you."

Tears welled in her eyes. "Me, too. For you."

She cleared her throat and wiped at the wetness on her cheeks. If she dwelled on this she'd never be able to leave this house, this room. And they had to. Soon.

She asked, "I'm assuming you didn't see who knocked you out or you'd have said so, right?"

"Right. I didn't even hear anything. The motor in the freezer was running. I just felt a sudden exploding pain through my skull, then nothing, until you were bending over me."

"So, who do you think was shooting at us tonight, er, last night?" She glanced at her watch, noting it was near dawn.

"I'm assuming it was the same person who hit me." Mark's expression turned puzzled and he shook his head. "But you know, since the person had a gun, why didn't whoever it was just shoot me?"

"Because he or she intended us to die in that freezer, intended it to look like a tragic accident. I don't think you were expected to awaken in time to tell me about the safety latch. But you did, and we escaped, and who-ever was there panicked."

"Who *could* it have been? Which of the three of them?"

"Four," she said. "Ali might have been involved. Not that I can assign her a motive at the moment, but she might once have been involved with Reese. Might still be. You saw them when we showed up unexpectedly."

"Okay, four. Which one is it?"

She considered. "Any of them, I suppose. I mean, Sookie and Ali didn't share with me any plans they might have had for the evening. Jay-Ray and Reese were supposedly meeting with clients at a Sonics' game, but they left in separate cars and either one of them could have doubled back. But we *can* ask if either of them was late getting to the game."

"All we'll have is their word for it. If it was Jay, Reese might have thought he was meeting with a woman or a bookie and alibi him."

"Jay would probably do the same for Reese."

"All Ali and Sookie have to do is lie. We won't know the difference." She wanted to scream with frustration.

"Maybe we'd better stick to following the money trail," Mark suggested.

"How are we supposed to do that? Where do we begin?" She sighed. "I feel like Dorothy looking for the start of the yellow brick road without the Munchkins to guide me. Do we somehow steal the keys to the office files? Maybe from Ali?"

He considered that a moment, then shook his head. "I don't think the Rayburns keep the kind of papers we need at the office. The home office where Wendy was killed is where we'll find what we're after."

"Return to the scene of the crime." Livia felt the

first stirring of hope. She'd heard that mentioned in every detective book or movie she'd ever read or watched. It made sense, if for no other reason than that it would give them a feel of what might have happened on that fatal afternoon three years ago. "We need access to the house. Maybe we should suggest a cocktail party or something to Sookie."

She could see from his face that he didn't like the idea.

He shoved his hand through his hair. "I'm afraid we couldn't steal away from a party—that I'd be catering and you'd be hosting—long enough to do what we need to do."

"You're probably right. So, what else?"

"I think it would be better if no one knows we're there."

"You mean...sneak in?" She could see it was exactly what he meant. "Okay, then I guess my question is, when do you want to do this?"

"Not today. We can't know whether or not one or more of our suspects might decide to come home and interrupt us. Besides, the servants will be there, too."

"Then when?"

"Tonight, after everyone has gone to bed."

"That's another whole day wasted, Mark." She tucked the hourglass and chain beneath her sweater. "Can we afford to wait?"

"We don't have any choice."

They stared at one another a long moment. Then Livia said, "Okay. Then, tomorrow, er, today, I'll arrange to pick Josh up from school, spend the afternoon with him at the mansion, and before I leave, I'll rig a door or window somehow for us to use to gain entry."

"Rig a door or window? My, you're becoming a real

B and E expert.'' He was grinning that devilish smile again. ''I hope nothing goes wrong. I'd hate to see your pretty little behind tossed in jail.''

''Don't even think that. I'm not going to land in jail. Besides, you'll be *breaking* and *entering* with me—be as much at risk of getting caught as me.''

''Well, that settles it, then. We can't get caught. I'm not going back to jail. Not even for you, pretty lady.''

The hourglass hanging over Livia's heart went icily cold.

Chapter Fourteen

LADY FINGERS

Take Some Motherly Wisdom
Spread It Over One Daughter
Stew Until Half Baked

The hourglass had never gone icy before, and Livia couldn't shake the awful sense that it was a portend of something bad, something worse than she had even imagined. She decided not to mention it to Mark. She headed home on near deserted streets, driving across town faster in the pre-rush-hour traffic than she should have, as though she could outrun whatever hovered on the horizon.

She sneaked into her parents' house half an hour before her mom got up to fix breakfast for her dad, a morning ritual every working day of his life.

As agitated as she felt, Livia didn't expect to sleep, but she realized she had when she awakened to the aroma of coffee. Still drowsy, she figured the scent wafted into her room through the heater vent as it had the other day.

A nearby noise startled her. She pried open her eyes

to find her mother sitting on a chair she'd pulled to the side of the bed. She held out a steaming mug for her. Livia jerked into a sitting position. "Is something wrong?"

"I thought maybe *you* could tell *me,* dear."

Livia struggled for control of her face. When Bev Kingston used her "mommy understands" voice, her "mommy understands" eyes on one of her kids, that kid was totally "found out." *I am in such trouble.*

Livia propped pillows at her back, wiped the sleep from her eyes, accepted the proffered mug and took a sip. The liquid rolled hot across her tongue and through her middle as scalding as the accusation in the set of her mother's double chins.

Despite this, Livia decided to play dumb as long as possible to figure out exactly what her mother knew. "What makes you think something is wrong with me, Mom?"

"Well, for one thing…you called to say you'd be out late, so naturally I assumed that meant you were with Reese. But then he called. So, obviously, you weren't with him."

"Reese called? When?"

How did this apple-cheeked matron in a pink polyester pantsuit, with her Shirley Temple curls and twinkling blue eyes manage to come across like a uniformed inquisitor? "Which time, dear?"

Which time? Reese had called more than once? How unlike him. "The first time."

"Around six."

Just after she and Mark had been shot at in the warehouse. "Reese and Jay-Ray were at a Sonics game at six, Mom. You must be mistaken about the time."

"No. Larry King had just come on. Six o'clock

sharp. Reese didn't mention anything about a basketball game. He said that his plans for the evening had changed and he was free to go to dinner with you and the boy."

Livia sipped coffee, pondering this. So, he and Jay-Ray's plans had changed. Had Jay gone on to the game without Reese? Or had they both skipped the game? Either way, one of them *could* have been the person shooting at her and Mark in the warehouse last night. She gave her mother a weak smile. "I'm sorry I missed a chance to be with Josh. I'm going to see him today, though."

"Where were you, dear?"

"Where did you tell him I was?" Livia drank more coffee.

Bev watched her. "I told him you had some things to take care of with Bridget. I figured that was where you were."

Good. "Thank you."

"He called again. Around nine."

"And…?"

"I told him you and Bridget had probably gone out to eat. He wondered why you didn't have your cell phone turned on. Why you weren't answering your voice mail. I don't mean this as criticism, dear, but you are usually—what's the word? Oh, yeah, anal—about that phone. About messages About everything. I don't know anyone as organized as you. So, something pretty important has to be going on for you to ignore that phone. To ignore your voice mail."

"I have a lot on my mind. A lot of planning and not a lot of days to do it in." She finger-combed her hair. "Bridget has been great about helping out."

She would have to talk to Bridget, get her to cover for her.

"Bridget called around ten," her mother said. "She hasn't seen you since before you had the flu."

So much for covering. Livia felt the blood draining from her face and decided she'd better stick as close to the truth as she could. Less chance of tripping herself up later. "I was planning the food. With the caterers."

"Until dawn?"

Mom had been checking this room half the night to see whether or not I was home. Livia groaned inwardly. How she had hated this trait in her mother before she'd moved out. This was exactly what she deserved for moving back in. No! *No, no, no, no.* She would never criticize this woman again for loving her or for being concerned about her. She'd been lucky to have been born into this big, nosy loving family. But she couldn't tell her mother the truth. Couldn't tell her that she might die in ten days...or less. "After I left the caterer's, I met with some of the gals from the gym."

Her mother's eyebrows arched. "Oh, there's an all-night health food bar someplace I don't know about?"

Livia winced at the sarcasm.

Her mother eyed her critically, the "understanding mommy" gone. "You're glowing, Livia. The kind of glow that a woman has who is well and truly in love."

"I am...in love." *Just not with my fiancé.* Livia blew out a breath, relieved that her mother didn't really know anything. She was guessing. Making assumptions without proof. "With Reese."

"Oh, really? Explain to me then why you've never had that glow in all these months. Not when you first announced you were marrying Reese Rayburn. Not when you brought him home to meet us. Not when he gave you his ring—a ring that is missing from your finger this morning."

Livia's gaze jerked to her hands. The ring. Oh, God, she'd left it on the toilet tank in Mark's bathroom. Her face burned as she lifted her gaze to her mother's. This was not good. Not good at all. Before she saw Reese or any of the Rayburns, or her family, she had to get that ring back on her finger where it belonged. "I left it in the bathroom."

Not *her* bathroom, but *a* bathroom. It was half true.

"Of all my brood, you were always the worst liar, Livia." Bev patted her cheek fondly as though she'd just paid her a supreme compliment. "I was going to mail your invitations today, but I'm not sure that's a good idea if there isn't going to be a wedding."

"There *is* going to be a wedding." Livia set the coffee on the nightstand, tossed aside the covers and strode to her dresser and yanked open the underwear drawer. "You're being silly, Mother. I look just the same as I always have."

Bev stood and put the chair back in the corner. "Then I should mail the invitations?"

Livia spun back to her mother, clutching clean panties and bra against her rapidly beating heart. "Would you mind waiting on that for a couple of days?"

"Of course not, dear...but why?"

Livia shrugged, gesturing as though it were no big deal. "I want to make sure no one's been forgotten."

"I see." Her mother gathered the mug Livia had discarded. "Meanwhile, I suggest you put your ring back on before you meet Reese for breakfast this morning."

Livia felt as if her stomach were one huge knot. "I'm not meeting Reese for breakfast."

"He seems to think you are. At least that's what he told me to tell you when he called around midnight."

The house phone rang.

"That's probably him now." Her mother looked as though she expected Livia to answer it.

"I can't talk to him. I—I have to shower. Could you get it?"

The phone kept ringing.

Her mother didn't move.

"Mom, please. If it *is* Reese, tell him I'm still sound asleep, that you haven't had a chance to speak to me yet."

Bev shook her head and folded her arms across her ample bosom. She abhorred lying and liars. No matter the cause. "Not unless you tell me what's going on."

"I can't. Not today. But soon. I promise."

Bev started toward the door with reluctance, then seemed to make up her mind about something and crossed to Livia, giving her cheek a sympathetic stroke. "Most every bride experiences a bout of cold feet, Livia, but if you're having sincere doubts, it is better to call the whole thing off than to say 'I do' to the wrong man. Marriage is more than a fancy-schmancy wedding. Too many women go into it with blinders on. They don't realize it's a lifelong commitment to clean up after some man, to share not endless hours of joy and passion, but day-to-day drudgeries. Choosing the wrong partner is like landing in hell. Choosing the right one..." She broke off, smiling. "Is a gift from heaven."

During her speech, the phone had stopped ringing. Livia stared at her mother, absorbing the sincerity of her words, understanding the partnership her parents shared as she never had before falling in love with

Mark. Tears filled her eyes at the realization that she and Mark might have nothing but the few remaining days to share.

Livia embraced her mother, hugging her tightly. "Thanks, Mom."

"For what?" Bev looked flustered. It wasn't like Livia to be sentimental and neither woman knew how to handle it.

Livia stepped back and gazed into her mother's eyes. "For everything."

The phone began to ring again, and Bev nodded, glancing between the shrill, insistent summons and her daughter, obviously torn. At last she made up her mind. "I'll catch the extension in the master bedroom."

As she watched her leave, Livia swallowed against the flutter of nerves in her stomach. She felt flustered, too. At her behavior, at the state of her world in general. She rushed into her bathroom, closing the door behind her. She had to get to Mark's, had to tell him that Reese and Jay-Ray were definitely on their suspect list after last night. She showered and dressed, frustrated and anxious, coming up with more questions than answers, all the while feeling time dwindling, slipping away.

Her mother was still talking on the phone as she let herself out the back door minutes later and tore to her car.

She wanted to phone Mark, but she dare not turn on her cell phone for fear Reese would call before she could dial. As she approached Cupid's Catering, she pulled into the alley, then thought better of it as she spied the van and a couple of cars occupying the parking area. Candee and Nanette were obviously inside and would be bound to wonder what a customer was doing pulling up to their back stoop.

She circled the block and parked in front of the house. She sprinted to the porch and rang the bell. She felt conspicuous and vulnerable on the open street, as if someone watched, spying on her. Though she hadn't noticed anyone—or any car anyway—following her *and* she'd been the only one parking as she pulled to the curb.

Nerves, she thought, chiding herself to calm down even as she gave the bell another impatient punch. Maybe the caterers didn't answer this door without an appointment. That was what their sign stated. She hugged her coat closer against a rising wind. How strict was their "appointment only" policy? Was business so good they could afford to lose foot traffic?

She shook off the erratic thoughts as she caught the sound of footsteps approaching from inside. The door opened and a petite natural blonde with waist-length hair secured in a ponytail and large unadorned brown eyes graced the doorway. She wore a T-shirt, ankle-length skirt, and earth sandals. Her teal apron was dusted with flour, reminding Livia of the flour that had dusted her jacket last night after the bullet split that bag on the shelf in the warehouse.

Her stomach clenched and the anxiety to get inside, out of harm's way, swept her anew. "I'm Livia Kingston, a client. I know I don't have an appointment, but I need to speak with Mr. Everett, if he's available." She half expected the woman to ask why she hadn't called if she had something to discuss with Mark.

But she smiled warmly. "I know who you are, Ms. Kingston. I'm Nanette White. Won't you come in. Mark's in the kitchen. I'll get him."

Nanette's professionalism spoke volumes. Whatever Mark had told his partners about them, the private stuff was still private. Between her and Mark. Her mother's words about spending her life with the right man came back to her and she knew she'd been fortunate to realize that Reese was not that man, but she was terrified of losing the one who was.

She heard voices in the kitchen and knew she could probably sneak up to his private living quarters without chance of interruption, but decided she didn't want Mark searching for her. She moved toward the fireplace, gazing at the love seats, her mind reeling with sensuous memories that quickened her pulse.

Mark came through the swinging door, wiping his hands on a towel. The sight of him spread warmth through her and eased her anxiety, despite the fact that his expression was tight, worried. She knew her showing up unexpectedly had alarmed him.

He rushed to her. "Is something wrong with Josh?"

"No."

"Did someone come after *you?*"

"No. I'm fine." She lowered her voice. "It's Reese. He wants to meet with me this morning and I left my engagement ring in your bathroom."

"Oh, God." Relief broke the tension in his face, and he caught her by the upper arms, grinning. "I'd hug you, but you're clean and as you can see, I've been cooking and sloppy with it, distracted by thoughts of you."

"Mark, listen to me, there's more—" But he cut her off, holding her slightly away from him, his lips finding hers, possessing hers. The hourglass heated against her breastbone. She sighed, every other thought slipping from her head as he released her. She murmured, "As

much as I'd like to follow that kiss to its natural conclusion, I haven't time. I need the ring.''

"Oh, yeah, Reese's ring.'' He scowled.

"Mark, he didn't go to the Sonics' game last night.
He called around six and left a message with my
mother about changing his plans and being free to take
Josh and me to dinner.''

Mark arched an eyebrow. "So, he has no alibi for
the time we were shot at?''

"No.''

"What about Jay-Ray?''

"I don't know.'' She shrugged. "I haven't returned
any of Reese's calls yet. But I'll find out over breakfast.''

The distress returned to Mark's face, and he grazed
her cheek with his knuckles. "Be careful what you say
to him.''

"Don't worry .''

"I can't help but worry about you. Now, where did
you say you left that ring?''

"On the toilet tank. On a piece of gauze like the one
on your head.'' She walked with him to the stairs,
touching the edges of his bandage making sure they
were secure. "How is your wound, by the way?''

"I haven't looked.'' He stopped, his grip on the ban-
ister, gazing down at her. "Maybe you should come
upstairs with me and check it.''

His smoldering gaze caressed her, and her mind and
body responded in kind. She sighed. "I know exactly
where that suggestion is meant to lead…right back to
your bed.''

He grinned his sinfully inviting grin.

She moaned, fighting the temptation swirling
through her. "Oh, Mark, we can't… Not right now…''

She nodded toward the kitchen, silently telling him that she wouldn't want Candee or Nanette coming upstairs to investigate strange noises issuing from his bedroom.

"Coward." He chuckled, kissing her nose. "I'll get the ring and bring it right down."

As she waited, Livia paced from the sitting area through the foyer and back to the staircase. What was taking so long? The nerves in her stomach seemed to be playing tetherball, and she kept pondering the fact that Reese had phoned so many times. It was unlike him. He'd called only three times during the whole week she'd spent in bed with the flu. But last night he'd called and called, as though it were urgent that he reach her. Truly odd. The only people who got that "urgent treatment" from him were clients.

So, why the urgency?

Was he the killer? The one who'd shot at them in the warehouse? If so, then he'd known where she was, who she was with. So why was he trying to reach her? Had he wanted to find out whether or not he'd managed to wound either or both of them?

Or had he been trying to reach her at all? Perhaps he intended the calls only to establish an alibi.

The thought sent shivers through her and she couldn't forget how cold the hourglass had felt. How very very cold.

A warning.

The door to Mark's private suite opened and she rushed to the bottom of the stairs. He shook his head. "I can't find it."

"What?" Disbelief drove her up the stairs toward him. "What do you mean, you can't find it?"

"It's not where you said. In fact, it's nowhere. Look for yourself."

She took the stairs two at a time. In the bathroom, she noted the things she'd used to attend to his wounds were in exactly the same places she'd left them. Everything but the ring. There was nothing on the gauze cloth. She shoved down a rising panic and dropped to her knees, searching around the base of the toilet, checking the back of the tank. No ring.

She rose and looked at him, puzzled. "I left it right on this piece of gauze. But it's not here anywhere."

"I swear *I* didn't touch it."

She shook her head at the idea that he would take it and hide it from her. He understood this wasn't a game they were playing. "I *know* that."

"I swear I didn't see it there this morning when I was in here, either."

"Well, if you didn't take it, and I didn't take it, who did? It couldn't have gotten up and walked away."

He scowled, puzzling the problem. "No one's been here but Candee and Nanette, and neither of them has been upstairs."

"Are you sure?"

"Positive."

Livia felt the hourglass turn icy again, as cold as the brick forming in her stomach. "Someone was here, Mark. While we were here. Someone took my ring."

"No way. The house was locked."

"Are you sure of that? You didn't check when we came in last night." She gazed at him pointedly. "I managed to get into this 'locked' house. Why couldn't someone else?"

"Maybe one of us knocked the ring into the toilet bowl during the night and didn't notice."

As much as she wanted to believe his explanation, she knew in her gut that it wasn't the right one. "If we had done that, the items on the tank would be disturbed, but everything is just as I left it and the gauze was at the back next to the wall. The ring would have had to slip past the tape and scissors and Mercurochrome to fall into the bowl. Someone had to have taken it or it would be *here*."

He wasn't convinced. He looked through the bathroom again.

She said, "Maybe we should check downstairs for signs of an intruder."

He gave her a that-would-be-a-waste-of-time look, but followed her downstairs without comment. The door to the washroom was ajar.

"Look," she whispered, her heart hammering.

Mark shook his head. "Candee or Nanette might have been in there this morning and forgotten to close the door tightly."

"But that's against policy," she reminded him, arguing further, "It has to be second nature to them to shut it all the way."

The door bumped against the jamb.

Livia started and stumbled back, her eyes rounding.

Mark stepped gingerly to the door and shoved it inward.

Damp winter wind blew in through the wide-open window.

Chapter Fifteen

RED HERRING GUMBO

Dice a Confusion of Clues
Into Heavy Speculation
Spice With a Fact or Two
Simmer All Day

Mark stalked to the window, lowered the sash, then swore. A circle had been cut from the glass right above the latch. He choked on the anger climbing his throat. He felt violated in a way he'd not thought possible. In prison he'd been subjected to every kind of humiliating experience man could inflict on man, but someone stealing into the house while he and Livia made love, spying on them, invading his private space, his privacy, his most intimate moments—that was the ultimate violation.

He barely restrained the urge to put his fist through what was left of the window as he turned to her. "I owe you an apology, Livia. We definitely had company last night."

She was the color of whipped egg whites. "Why didn't we hear anything?"

The answer to that was obvious and fueled his blazing resentment. But he gave her face a gentle caress. "We were otherwise engaged, darlin'."

She nuzzled his hand and blew out a shaky breath.

He glanced at the window again and stifled another curse. Entry had been simple enough, requiring little expertise. Remove the glass, reach in and undo the lock. "Candee and Nanette begged me to put in a hi-tech alarm system, but I wouldn't do it. I didn't want to deal with cops of any kind, not even rent-a-cops. Hell, I figured the worst intruder we'd get was some teenager after something to sell for drug money. I mean, sure the kitchen equipment is worth big bucks, but anyone wanting that would be specialized, and career thieves would come with a big truck and clean us out in minutes, with or without an alarm system."

A blast of wind howled eerily through the hole in the glass.

Livia lifted the collar of her jacket, framing that angelic face he loved to kiss. She said, "I'd have thought after being shot at you'd rethink your stance on electronic alarms."

"I didn't have to. My partners took a dim view of the bullet hole in the kitchen window. We've arranged for one of the best systems on the market, but the installation had to be fit into the schedule. It should be installed by this time next week." He plowed his fingers through his hair. "If I'd listened to them to begin with instead of being pigheaded, whoever did this last night might be in lockup this morning."

"Stop beating yourself up."

"I can't help it. Every minute this goes on, people I care about are in jeopardy."

She caught his hand and made him look at her,

speaking low, "But *were* we in jeopardy last night? Were we really?"

He locked gazes with her, glad to see color returning to her face. "What do you mean?"

"If the person who shot at us in the warehouse was here last night, why are we still walking around?"

"I don't know." He considered that, then shook his head. "It doesn't follow, does it?"

She worried her lower lip, glancing pointedly at the window. "Is there any clue as to whom it might have been, Mark?"

He studied the frame with renewed interest. "Just a scrape on the sill that seems to have been made by a heavy heel."

"A man." She hugged herself.

"Probably."

The tetherball game restarted in her stomach with the fever of an overtime playoff. "You think it was Reese?"

"I don't know." He shrugged, his black brows coming together in a frown. "I don't understand why, if it was Reese, he didn't confront us, or kill us."

She thought about that a moment. "Remember what you said about prime suspects?"

He nodded. "Sort of."

She hugged herself against another blast of chilly air, and continued, "If we were found together murdered in your bed, Reese would be the first one the police would suspect and if he didn't have an airtight alibi, he'd be arrested and charged as fast as you were. In other words, if he *did* kill Wendy and framed you, he wouldn't commit a murder that pointed to himself."

Mark motioned for her to leave the bathroom and closed the door, cutting off the damp breeze. "After failing to kill us in the freezer in what would likely have appeared to be some sort of tragic accident, why didn't the person firing at us in the warehouse finish us off there and then? I mean, he shot out the lights and fired a few bullets over our heads, but was he trying to hit us? Or kill us? He had a flashlight and a gun. He could have found us and finished us off. Instead, he ran."

She considered this. "You think he was showing us he can take us out whenever he wants?"

"And wherever he wants."

"So, he's also striving to avoid a homicide investigation?"

"This time, yes. Certainly one that leads to Rayburn Grocers."

Livia reached to touch the hourglass through the layers of clothing, the solid lump of it somehow reassuring. Something still didn't make sense. *I was shot with a bullet meant for Mark. The Processor said as much. Said if I was shot again, instead of Mark, I'd have to be processed into Heaven even if it wasn't my time.*

But if the killer didn't intend for Mark to die by gunshot, how had she come to be shot in his place? Did that mean they would push the killer to such desperation he or she would use a gun even though it would stir an investigation? Or had the method of murder, as well as the time frame, been altered as she'd feared by her falling in love with Mark, leaving them totally clueless and vulnerable to whatever vile accident awaited them?

Mark intruded on her dark thoughts. "So, if murder wasn't the motive for breaking in here last night, what was? Surely not robbery. Whoever took your ring couldn't have known it wouldn't be on your finger."

The question sent her thoughts scurrying and her gaze winging to his. Was he wrong? *Could* theft have been the motive? "Is anything missing besides my ring?"

"Nothing obvious, that's for damn sure—or my partners or I would have noticed it this morning."

Livia inhaled deeply, catching the delicious aromas of baking pastries, something with strawberries and— An awful thought struck her. She caught Mark's arm.

His eyes narrowed. "What?"

"Last night when I came down here and got the cider, chocolate and strawberries, I noticed one of the knives was missing from the oak butcher block. It looked like a large one."

"A knife? You think someone took one of my knives?" Alarm lit his golden eyes. "Dear God, you think he intends to frame me for another murder?"

"Is that so farfetched?"

"Hell, I hope so." He spun away from her and into the kitchen.

Livia followed. Here the wonderful scents smashed together in a delight of fragrances, treats for Valentine's Day. But instead of making her mouth water, the sweet aromas tightened the knot in her stomach. Candee was extracting a sheet of heart-shaped cookies from the oven as Nanette sat on a tall stool rolling out dough. Both glanced up, but neither seemed surprised to see one of their customers barging in on them while they worked.

Mark went to the counter where the butcher block stood. It was empty. A pulse throbbed in his neck as he pointed at it. "Are all of the knives in the dishwasher?"

"I suppose." Candee set the cookie sheet down beside a bowl of red frosting and glittery sprinkles. "I ran a load earlier. Should be done by now."

Mark opened the dishwasher, grabbed the silverware catcher free, then began jamming each knife into its respective slot, stabbing the blades to the hilt, a sure sign of the tangle of emotions she knew he was fighting.

He cursed. "It's not here."

"What's not there?" Nanette scowled, alarmed at Mark's behavior.

"Yes," Candee agreed. "What's up, Big E?"

Mark filled them in on the break-in and the possible reason for it.

"That's it," Nanette said, brushing her small hands together and sending flour flying as she stood. "I'm calling the police and reporting this."

"Please, don't." Mark stood with one hand gripping the solid chrome handle of the largest knife.

Candee shook his head. "We respect that you don't want to be questioned by law enforcement officers, Big E, but do you not see the wisdom of having some sort of report on record should it later be necessary?"

Mark exchanged glances with Livia, and she knew exactly what he was wrestling with. She nodded for him to go ahead and tell them. He cleared his throat. "I wasn't alone last night. And if the police come they'll want a statement from both Livia and me. That could cause us more problems than it solves."

Livia felt her cheeks warm, but she lifted her chin. She wasn't ashamed of the way she felt about Mark, didn't mind that his partners knew. She wished she could tell the whole world. Could break off her engagement with Reese and stop sneaking around. But that might never happen.

Neither Candee nor Nanette seemed shocked by Mark's revelation, or judgmental, either.

They shared a look, shrugged and nodded. Candee said, "We won't call the police."

"This time," Nanette added.

"Thank you." Livia realized she was trembling. "I have to go, Mark."

He followed her to the foyer.

She said, "Reese expects me to meet him for breakfast. He'll wonder why I'm not returning his calls."

Mark caught her by the upper arms and kissed her hard and long, then he gazed into her eyes, and she knew he was as reluctant to release her as she was to be released.

He said, "I wish you wouldn't meet him."

She breathed in his vanilla scent and memories of the night before flooded her, threatening to rob her resolve to go. "I have to. If he's not the killer, he'll wonder why I'm avoiding him. I don't want to stir up trouble where none exists."

"If he is the killer, you're at risk every time you're alone with him."

The concern in his eyes fed her own worries. But she refused to give in to the paranoia. "He won't try anything in a public restaurant."

"What are you going to tell him about the ring?"

She rubbed at her naked finger. "I don't know. I'll think of something like…like…like it's at the jeweler's…that one of the prongs broke and had to be replaced."

"That's good. Believable." He nodded. "Unless he stole it."

She tightened her hold on her hand. "Why would he steal the ring? Why not leave it where it was?"

"To play games with you. To watch you squirm."

"I thought Wendy was the one who liked to do that?" she said it gently, but he winced.

"Oh, I don't know." He jammed his hand through his hair. "It's no secret that I don't like the man. Or that he dislikes me equally. But one thing I do know about Reese is that he wouldn't come at me for a physical confrontation. Fisticuffs aren't his style. He'd do what the killer is doing—sneak attacks."

"We have to get this solved, Mark."

"Maybe we'll get lucky tonight."

"I pray you're right."

BUT WERE PRAYERS ENOUGH? Livia wondered as she drove to Jane's Gym. No, she couldn't dwell on what lay ahead of them tonight. She had enough to contend with just getting through the day. She hadn't been to work in two weeks, was lucky to have an understanding boss, but even Jane's patience had limits. As much as she'd like to expend some of her edginess in a wild aerobic workout or two, Livia wasn't slated to lead any classes for the next couple of days; but she had to get back on the schedule or lose her job.

She supposed losing her job should be the least of her worries, considering everything else that was on the line. But it made a great excuse for getting out of breakfast with Reese. She didn't speak to him, but left a message with Ali, asking her to pass along that she'd meet him for dinner around six tonight. Next, she called the Rayburn mansion and told the chauffeur she'd pick up Josh after school today.

If the weather didn't turn nasty, she planned on taking him to the park. She'd bet he needed to kick his soccer ball as badly as she did.

The gym was crowded, clients on every exercise machine, in the aerobic classes and locker areas as Livia hustled inside and found her boss. Jane was even more generous than usual, insisting Livia take as many days as she needed, promising her job would still be there when she returned from her honeymoon.

But the last thing Jane said was, "Call your fiancé. He's driving the staff nuts with his messages."

Livia rolled her eyes and strode to her own office. She checked her voice mail, some twenty plus, and began listening. Each time she heard Reese's voice, she hit the skip button. She couldn't deal with him at the moment. No matter what he wanted.

She stayed at Jane's long enough to do some paperwork, and to say hi to some of her co-workers, then she drove to the Bread and Brew to get some homemade vegetable soup, a whole-wheat muffin, and some sisterly contact. It was nearly lunchtime, but as busy as she was, Bridget took the time to join her at one of the ice-cream-parlor tables. It smelled almost as wonderful in here as in Mark's kitchen, certainly better than the gym. Livia dug into the food, relishing the mix of flavors and textures.

Bridget dropped onto the chair across from her. Her normally twinkly blue eyes studied Livia as she tucked a strand of wayward dark hair behind one ear. "Mom said you had a glow and she's right. What's up with you?"

"Bridget, you wouldn't believe it even if I could tell you and I can't tell you."

Her sister leaned closer to her. "You used to tell me everything."

Livia laughed. "I did not."

"Well, maybe you should have."

"Yeah, maybe I should have." She set her spoon down and covered her sister's hand with her own.

Bridget looked startled. "Are you sick or something?"

"I just want you to know that you're the best. I don't think I ever told you and I'm not sure you know it, but I want you to."

"What did you do?" Bridget's eyebrows were reaching toward her hairline. "Spend all of last week pretending to have the flu while secretly listening to tapes of Dr. Phil?"

Livia bit down a grin. "A person could do worse than take Dr. Phil's advice."

Bridget just kept staring at her, obviously puzzled.

Livia finished her soup, then went to the counter to pay. "You'd better give me one of your tuna fish sandwiches, that giant oatmeal-raisin cookie, and a milk to go."

It was Josh's favorite takeout food. Livia blinked as the thought crossed her mind. Since she'd known him, she couldn't recall anyone ever taking Josh to a fast-food restaurant or bringing him home a fast-food meal. Not that she approved of eating greasy fries and fatty hamburgers, but all the same…it was an experience every kid should have.

Reese would have a fit, but tonight for dinner, they were going somewhere totally kid-oriented.

Josh's face glowed when he spotted her waiting for him. "Livia!"

He rushed into her arms and she lifted him and swung him around. She wouldn't always be allowed to do this. But he was still young enough that kisses and hugs didn't embarrass him. However, it wouldn't last. Other boys his age shoved their parents away.

Other boys weren't as lonely as Josh.

Pity stabbed her heart. He seemed thinner than he had a week and a half ago, pale, too. Did no one in the Rayburn house pay any attention to him? God, he needed his father. Needed him badly. They *had* to solve Wendy's murder. Not just for Mark and her, but for this little boy who seemed to be wasting away, feeling abandoned and all but friendless, unwanted and unloved in the only home he'd ever known.

She set him down, peering into his freckled face. He looked, she suspected, much as his mother might have looked at his age.

She said, "I thought we'd go to the park today, have a little picnic and afterward, kick around your soccer ball. Would you like that?"

"I guess. What did you bring to eat?"

"Bridget packed your favorites."

"Goodie."

She didn't make him wait to dig into the food until they were at the park, but handed him the sack and let him unwrap the cookie first to take a bite. Crumbs could always be vacuumed from the seats, but his delight would stay with her always. And then with a jolt of realization, it dawned on Livia what she'd been doing all morning, with her mother, with Jane and her co-workers, with Bev and Josh. She was saying goodbye.

In case she couldn't stop the murderer from killing her again, she was using this second chance Heaven had given her to tell the special people in her life goodbye.

Chapter Sixteen

SILVER DOLLAR COOKIES

Mix the Dough
Roll the Dough
Follow the Dough

Mark spent a miserable morning picturing Livia at breakfast with Reese, worrying that he was the killer. *That she was in trouble.* That he wasn't the killer. *That she was in trouble.* That he'd taken the ring and confronted her with it. *That she was in trouble.*

His mood went from dour to sour and by afternoon, he knew he had to see for himself or go crazy. But seeing and being seen were two different things. The Cupid's Catering van was too conspicuous. Especially on the evening before Valentine's Day. He borrowed Candee's black Toyota Tacoma. The dashboard looked like something out of a Star Wars movie. His partner had ripped out all of the stock gauges and installed new, ultra-sleek digital ones, along with special speakers and a hi-tech stereo system.

Shaking his head, Mark started the motor. Hip-hop rap blasted through the pickup cab. He slapped his hands over his ears. Where the hell was the off button? The music kept assaulting as he desperately spun knobs, punched buttons. As suddenly as it blared, the volume quieted to a tolerable level, but he couldn't figure out how to turn it off or how to eject the CD or to switch to a different one.

The bass beat seemed to march to the drum of his nerves, bouncing his mind back to Livia.

He recalled she planned to pick up Josh from school. Had she taken him to the mansion or somewhere else? He could hardly drive up to the gates of Rayburn Roost—the Rayburn Estate—and ask. He drove past the Bread and Brew, then on a whim, went in. He ordered a coffee to go from Bridget and discussed the wedding cake, segueing to the subject of Livia.

"She was in here a while ago," Bridget confided. "Took a picnic lunch for Josh. I think they were going to the park."

Mark thanked her and took off. He hoped the park Bridget mentioned was the same one Livia had taken the boy to the other day and went there first. Spotting her compact in the parking lot, Mark sucked in his first worry-free breath in hours.

Even though she wasn't likely to know this pickup, he deliberately parked several cars from hers and exited into the wooded area that ran along this section to the lake.

He heard them before he saw them, recognizing those two delightful laughing voices entwined on this crisp winter afternoon in that magical way one recognizes the primary notes of a favorite melody sung by favorite performers. He stopped as they came into view. The angel with the twinkling eyes and warm heart. The little boy with the cupid smile and eyes that were too old for any kid with only six years under his belt. Forget the Seven Wonders of the World. This was the most incredible sight to fill any man's gaze. And heart.

He leaned against a tree, peering through the branches, contenting himself with watching. He ached to let them know he was there, ached to hold his boy for what might prove the last time. But he dare not. Not without telling Josh who he was—and doing that would be too cruel. Especially if he died in a few days.

Josh laughed and gave the ball a hard kick. It flew between the stones they'd set up as goal posts and he squealed with delight. "I score! That's three points for me. None for you. I rock!"

Livia caught him by the shoulders, hugging him, beaming at his joy, and Mark felt warmth spread through his chest. Anyone could see how much she cared for Josh and Josh for her. It was the one truth that kept the agony of leaving them both behind from destroying him. He knew wherever he spent eternity that these memories would help him through the loneliness without Livia and Josh. That the two people he loved most in this world would have each other to cling to. Always.

He'd made sure of it. He'd spoken to his lawyer, had had papers drawn up naming Livia as Josh's guardian, granting her full custody of his son. He had also taken out a huge insurance policy on his life with Livia the beneficiary, money he knew she would probably need to battle the Rayburn attorneys in court if Wendy's family decided to fight her for Josh. He prayed they wouldn't, prayed that there really was a God in Heaven, as Livia claimed, and that she could use the money instead to raise his son.

A dark form shifted among the trees directly across the open area where Livia and Josh played. Mark's body tensed, his nerves on full alert. Animal? Or human? His gaze delved the dense cover. There. A flash of something dark, black against the green leaves and brown tree trunks. A person. Someone else watching Livia and the boy. Mark stifled the urge to shout a warning that would not only give away the other person's presence, but his own.

He pinpointed the spot in his mind, ducked down and began moving through the trees with the stealth of a stalking jaguar, muscles taut, eyes vigilant. Sidestepping twigs and litter, he placed his feet with care. Purpose. His pulse banged. He stopped, strained to hear above the roar in his ears, the noise Livia and Josh were making. It was useless.

He could hear nothing.

But if he charged ahead, the clatter he raised would be heard by all.

Wrestling the temptation to rush, he placed one foot in front of the other and kept on. Dampness dropped off the trees and onto his head. Into his eyes. He batted it away, silently cursing. When he reached the spot where he'd seen the other watcher, it was deserted. Where the hell had he gone? Mark squatted and examined the flattened, crushed leaves around him, seeking a clue of some sort. Nothing. Damn it. Not even a clear footprint.

As he rose, he studied his surroundings. He'd made a half circle around the open picnic area where Livia and Josh played. He was near the parking lot. Had the watcher taken off for his car? Or was he still around somewhere? Still spying on Livia and Josh? Mark scoured the woods, back to the area where he'd stood originally. Nothing moved.

An unsettling shiver tracked his spine.

Where the hell was the watcher now?

He caught the slam of a car door above Josh's laughter, the noise like a sour note in an otherwise sweet concerto. Mark ran to the parking lot, arriving just as a dark sedan raced off. It was too far away for him to see the license number, but didn't have *that* much of a head start. He dragged the keys from his pocket and leaped into the pickup. "You aren't going to get away from me this time, you bastard."

He peeled out of the lot after the sedan, his foot slamming as hard as the music issuing from the speakers. He glimpsed the dark car ahead of him. About three blocks, he judged, smiling. "Your luck has finally run out."

As though its driver had heard him, the sedan sped ahead, dodging from one lane to the next. Mark followed suit, whipping through traffic at unsafe and illegal speeds. The sedan did the same, maintaining the gap between them, perhaps gaining a car length.

At the intersection, the dark car charged up the steep winding hill, past the gravel pit and onto the Sammamish Plateau. The road wound by high-end and cheapend housing developments clustered like mushrooms sprung from this once fertile and wildly wooded area. Here, traffic moved slower, but passing was impossible given the high volume traveling both directions.

It struck him that they were driving toward Rayburn Roost.

Mark kept his gaze pinned to the dark sedan, still savoring the sense that he'd know in a few minutes who it was who'd broken into his house and stolen Livia's ring.

Without warning, the SUV in front of him stopped dead in the road.

"No!" Mark, riding the guy's bumper, slammed the brake pedal with both feet. He braced for collision. The tires grabbed and squealed. The seat belt bit into him. The pickup bucked. Then skidded sideways. Missing impact by centimeters.

Mark cursed out a stream of fowl words on a gust of relieved breath. Then groaned as he realized the SUV driver had stopped to wave a school bus into line in front of them. The bus cut off the view ahead. There were no children aboard. It wouldn't be starting and stopping. Nonetheless, Mark smacked the dashboard with his fist. Traffic started moving again and he pulled over the yellow line again and again, but couldn't find a place to pass. By the time the bus turned into a schoolyard, the dark sedan was nowhere in sight.

Where the hell had it gone? His gut knotted, and rage the likes of which he'd felt the day he was sentenced to life imprisonment started deep in his belly, burning up through his body. Where the hell had it gone?

He came upon a shopping center, angled in, and circled the large parking lot. Twice. Several dark sedans occupied spaces, but he didn't see the one he'd been following. He pulled to the curb, shut off the truck, and slapped the steering wheel, trying to figure out what he should do next. Return to the park? Wait here, hoping the sedan came back this way?

What were the chances of that?

The knot in his gut tightened as he glanced around, realizing he was close to Rayburn Roost. Had the person driving the black sedan gone there as he'd thought they might? Should he go and find out? He mulled the pros and cons of showing up at the mansion unexpectedly, and decided he needed some sort of excuse. But what? He sighed as the answer came. He had the perfect excuse. The wedding was being held at the mansion. He was the wedding caterer. He needed to look around to know what supplies he would be required to bring.

Smiling, Mark started the pickup.

RAYBURN ROOST stood in the center of five wooded acres, one of the few remaining undeveloped stretches of land left on the plateau. Built in the fifties, the two-story, redbrick mansion had been designed with four separate wings upstairs so that the Rayburns could marry and live under one roof, offering their spouses, if not the real thing, at least the *sense* of privacy. The main floor—living room, formal dining room, kitchen, library and study—were shared by all.

Entrance was blocked by an electronic gate with a coded keypad. He could see the house well enough from here, but there was no dark sedan parked on the circular drive. If it was here, it would be around back, in or near the ten-car garage. He had to know.

Had the sedan been parked out front, he would have stuck to his plan to drive up to the front door and explain that he was there about catering the wedding. But *that* would not get him into the garage. He had to enter covertly. Getting into the grounds was no big deal. Though the front easement was gated, the only fence surrounding the perimeter was a natural border of firs and shrubs.

He drove to the next street, some four blocks away,

and returned on foot. A hundred yards from the gate, he cut into the treeline and made for the garage.

Thunder rumbled in the distance. A wall of gunmetal clouds rolled across the sky, dragging cold wind in its wake, stripping the afternoon of daylight. Eerie shadows popped up everywhere, as though specters skipped through the gardens. Mark hoped he seemed one of them, darting from shrub to bush as furtively as a soldier approaching enemy territory.

The garage had living quarters upstairs for the chauffeur. Lights shone through those windows. He dashed to the back edge of the long garage, then crept toward the front, figuring to find a few of the bays open. But the doors had been closed against the brewing storm, and there was no dark sedan or any other car parked on the blacktopped tarmac.

He would have to get into the garage. He eyed the lighted windows above, wishing he knew whether the chauffeur was upstairs or down. He didn't want to encounter any of the servants or the family members.

But I have to know whether or not that dark sedan is there.

He retreated and circled around the back of the garage to the other end, to the side door. Just as he reached it, it swung outward, knocking into his hand. He scrambled back around the end of the building.

A man ordered, "Vacuum it, fill it with gas and have it parked in front in half an hour."

Jay-Ray.

A second, unfamiliar male voice answered, "Yes, Mr. Rayburn."

Jay Rayburn's heels hit the tarmac like a colonel's march step as he struck off to the house. The chauffeur caught the door and began pulling it inward. Mark hurried to peer in before he shut it completely. Through the crack along the hinged edge, he saw it. The dark sedan.

Had Jay-Ray been driving it?

His pulse raced as he flattened himself against the garage wall, itching to go inside and feel the hood, knowing he couldn't. The door clicked shut at the same moment the storm burst, pummeling down great large drops of rain.

Mark darted for the house, not certain what he was going to do. How he would get in.

His nerves felt scraped and raw.

His gut knotted.

This house. This damned house.

As he started past the office window, the desk lamp flicked on. Voices came from within. He pressed himself against the brick wall. He couldn't make out what was being said, or discern who was speaking. He risked a glance inside, but as his eyes came level with the glass, the drapes came together, cutting off his view.

He had to get inside. Now. But how? He considered, then decided to enter through the sunroom since in the past it was the first door unlocked each morning and the last locked each night. Moments later, he was standing amid six-foot rubber plants and an array of wicker furniture.

Mark knew this house like the back of his scarred hand. Had peered into every mean nook and cranny. Had paced every vast and lonely expanse. He hated being here. Hated his son being here. He clamped his jaw and stole into the hallway leading to the study. His legs felt heavy, leaden. Damn. What was wrong with him? He inhaled and the familiar scent of lemon oil and aged wallpaper wrapped around him—the aroma

alive in his memory. It was being in this house. Ghosts.
Too many ghosts. His scowl tightened and a nerve in
his neck throbbed.

He pushed on, sneaking along the carpeted hallway,
ears keen. The office door stood ajar and he could see
the edge of a framed poster that hung over the desk.
The room held several such photos, all of Jay-Ray during his brief stint on the Sonics' roster. The furniture
was polished leather in a rusty-brown color that reminded Mark of dried autumn leaves. A masculine
room full of testosterone whether any man occupied it
or not.

An odd room for Wendy to have died in.

As he neared, he heard male voices and smashed
himself against the wall, listening.

"—her trust fund," Reese said. His tone sharpened
and faded as though he paced when he spoke, moving
closer then farther away from the door. "—assumed
our lawyers were handling. But when I questioned
Sloan today, he told me that you were the executor of
first Wendy's money and now the boy's."

"It wasn't a secret," Jay-Ray said. "I began man-
aging all of the money, including Wendy's, when Phillip's heart condition left him bedridden."

"Why?"

"He asked me to."

Neither man spoke for a moment and during the
tense silence, Mark wished he could see into the room,
read their faces, their body language, which he expected would tell him even more than what they were
saying.

"As I understand it," Reese said. "Wendy couldn't
touch the money in that trust fund until she turned

twenty-six, which happened to be the day before she died.''

"Not a trust fund, Reese. When I took over I realized it was a waste for all that money to just sit there when it could grow. I put the funds into diversified stocks. Investments. Built her a solid portfolio.''

"Oh?'' Reese sounded surprised. "I expect it's a lot larger now than it was three years ago, then.''

"Odds are against you there, pal,'' Jay-Ray said. "The stock market is always a gamble. It's taken some bad hits lately. A lot of stocks are down. Some more so than others. Even some that were considered solid investments. We've suffered a bit, as you know. Couldn't be helped.''

"But the boy's money is safe. In CDs and things, right?''

Mark's mouth dried. He couldn't have scripted this better if he'd tried. He wondered if Heaven had had a hand in putting him here to hear this.

"Well...no.'' Jay-Ray gave a nervous laugh. "Not all of it.''

"I'd like to look at the whole bunch. I'm going to be adopting the kid and taking over the handling of his money as soon as the adoption is finalized.''

"Really, Reese, I find that a bit insulting.''

"Don't take it personally, Jay.'' Reese's assurance dripped honey. "It's strictly business.''

Jay-Ray's voice rose and leather squeaked as though he'd raised halfway out of his desk chair. "You bet I take it personally.''

"I don't know why,'' Reese said. "You wouldn't be handling that money now if Wendy was still alive.''

Though Mark stood in the hall, he felt the chill that had fallen over the office.

"Haven't you ever wondered why Ethan killed her here...in this room...with his own knife?" Reese's voice faded then grew stronger again, as though he'd resumed pacing.

"No. I didn't want to dwell on the details then, and I damn sure don't want to do so now. I don't want those gruesome images in my mind every time I use this room. I can't imagine that you do, either."

Reese kept on. "I mean, if he was going to leave a weapon that pointed directly to him, why not do it at the restaurant?"

"How in hell should I know? You can't bet on what a killer will do."

"True, but I have wondered—"

"There's nothing to wonder about. Ethan killed your sister in a fit of rage. End of story. I don't understand why you're bringing it up now."

"Just thinking of Josh's inheritance—which naturally brings Wendy to mind." Reese sounded apologetic. "Where do you keep the records?"

"At the office. On my computer."

"Okay. Good. I'll want to look at them in the morn—" He broke off and when he spoke again his voice had changed. "What the hell is this?"

Mark fought the urge to move closer to the door, to peer inside.

"Looks like an envelope to me," Jay-Ray drawled.

"Yes," Reese's annoyance was palpable. "But how did it get into my jacket pocket?"

Over the ripping of paper, Mark caught the *slap-slap* of backless pumps. The second sound was not coming from the office, but from the hall leading into this one. He jerked away from the wall and took off in the other direction. He stopped long enough to unlatch one of the sunroom windows as extra insurance for Livia and his planned break-in later that night. But he doubted they would need it since the information they sought was kept at Rayburn Grocers. He ran out the way he'd come in.

The cool rain felt good on his heated face, energizing, refreshing, vitalizing. He started to sprint across the garage tarmac that separated the backyard and the perimeter gardens. One of the bays opened, spilling light into the stormy evening. Mark stood stone-still as the chauffeur drove the black sedan toward the front of the house.

Follow the money. The money had lead to Jay Rayburn—Jay-Ray who also drove the dark sedan.

He had to get hold of Livia to figure out what to do next. Mark rushed back to the truck. And slammed inside. The keys. Where had he put them? He poked on an overhead reading light and plunged his hand into his pants' pocket. That was when he noticed the card-size envelope on the seat—with his name written on it.

Mark felt a shiver through his belly. He tore open the seal and dragged out a single slip of paper. It was a crudely scrawled note.

Where is your son, Ethan? Your whore? Are they still at the park? Or do I have them now?

Chapter Seventeen

DEATH BY CHOCOLATE

Cocoa
Mocha
Double Dark Fudge
To Die For

Thunder rumbled across the sky, the vibration like a hand stroke on Livia's nerves. The tension she'd expended playing with Josh had eased the knots in her muscles, but not the sense that time was running out. She wished she could call Mark, hear his voice, spend whatever hours she had left with him and his son, see the two males she loved most in the world interacting, laughing, playing, connecting.

She glanced at the little boy beside her and knew this was a wish she could grant herself, but at what cost to him? He didn't know Mark was his daddy. Hadn't seen his daddy for three years, hadn't spoken to him, hugged him, kissed him. Sorrow for both the man and the child lay heavy against her heart. She would give anything to share in their eventual reunion.

But as surely as her car's windshield wipers were

inadequate against the pounding rain, she knew that was not to be. Knew that for Wendy's murderer to be found she, Livia, or Mark, would have to die.

"When are we gonna have dinner with Reese?" Josh asked.

"Tonight."

"I know. Nana Sookie told me. But when? I'm hungry."

"I guess we should call Reese and ask." In case Josh could see her face in the light cast from passing cars, she produced a smile she didn't feel, grimacing inside at the idea of finally speaking to Reese. She gathered a breath and tugged her cell phone from her purse. It trembled in her hand. She shot a glance at the readout. Hadn't she turned it off this morning? *No.* It appeared she'd only put it on mute and now the battery was fading fast. "Well, Mr. Josh-man, looks like we're going to have to go to the house to find out what's up with dinner tonight because my phone is dead."

"Dead? Like my mommy?"

"Oh, no, honey." Livia blanched at the pain in his voice, at her thoughtless choice of words. Her stomach twisted at the realization that she, too, might soon be dead, the second mother figure in his life to abandon him. *God, please don't hand him more trauma than he can take. He's just a little kid.*

She patted his hand. "I meant the battery has run out of power and needs to be recharged. But that will take an hour or two."

He gripped her hand in both of his before she could pull it back. "Can we go to dinner by ourselves?"

"You mean, just you and me?"

He nodded hard, and she supposed she couldn't blame him. Reese strictly enforced rules of etiquette no matter where they ate; she knew being constantly corrected was never fun for a child. Maybe she was being sentimental or nostalgic, but she wanted to remember Josh with a smile on his darling face, not the tension Reese could cause him.

Reese would be furious.

Tough!

She said, "I have an idea. How would you like to go for hamburgers and French fries?"

"Wow. Really, Livia? Can we?"

"We can do anything we want." She considered all of the fast-food places she drove past daily and decided on one that she'd noticed also had a children's play area inside.

At the restaurant, Josh became a child transformed. He shed his usual sullen shyness, joined other children in the plastic tube, came to the table and dug into his hamburger, fries and orange pop, then returned to romp again through the play area. After he'd eaten most of his meal, she treated him to an ice cream cone.

"This was the most fun I ever had, Livia. Can we do it again tomorrow? Please..." He had a thin orange moustache, ketchup stains on his shirt, and a smile as bright as one of the lightning bolts knifing the sky. She wished Mark was with them, sharing this moment, seeing his son's delight. How it would warm his heart.

Waiting until midnight to be with Mark suddenly seemed too far away.

As she drove to the Sammamish Plateau, she decided, once Josh was securely home, and she'd faced down Reese's ire, she would go to Mark's and spend the rest of the evening with him. Traffic was slow and cautious on the rainy streets, but they arrived safe and sound.

She saw Josh into the house.

"Well, look what the cat finally dragged in." Sookie's heels slapped the marble foyer floor like the rat-a-tat of a woodpecker's beak hitting bark. In a solid red jumpsuit, her topknot flopping with each step, her narrow face tight and accusing, she resembled that very bird. "Where have you had my grandson? He looks as though he's been rooting in a pig patch. Josh, Nanny has your bath ready. You go on up."

Josh gave Livia a hug and she felt her heart breaking, knowing she'd never hug this child again. She clung to him fiercely for the beat of five seconds, kissed him, then whispered, "Thanks for a wonderful time, Josh-man. I love you so much."

"I love you too much, too."

Livia released him, grinning at his words, fighting back tears.

As the little boy ran toward the stairs, she turned back to Sookie. She hadn't been mistaken about the anger in her eyes. Livia had been prepared for Reese's ire, not his mother's. She decided to ignore it, if possible. "Is Reese here?"

"No. He's not."

"Well, then, I guess he was going to cancel our dinner date himself, so it's just as well that Josh and I went alone."

Sookie huffed, her lean body tensing as if she'd been insulted. "Reese had planned on meeting you for dinner tonight, but he couldn't reach you. Anywhere."

"I didn't mean to be 'unreachable.' I had my phone, but not on my person. I left it in the car while Josh and I were at the park and the battery died."

Sookie just stared at her, not buying the excuse.

"You seem upset, Sookie. I hope it has nothing to do with the wedding preparations."

"You should know."

Livia lifted her eyebrows. "Well, I don't. So, why don't you spare me a dozen guesses and tell me out-right?"

"Why is my grandson such a mess?" Sookie asked. "I took him for a hamburger and some fries. Did you know he's never had that before?"

"You, of all people, should know saturated fat is the worst thing you can feed a child." Sookie pursed her carmine-slathered lips. "You ought to be ashamed, but I suppose trash like you doesn't know the feeling."

Trash like you. "Excuse me?" Shock smacked Livia. "What are you talking about?"

Sookie's gaze slid to Livia's left hand and suddenly Livia knew what this was all about. "Where is that lovely engagement ring my son gave you?"

Livia had the distinct feeling that Sookie knew ex-actly where it was, but she swallowed over the growing lump in her throat and lied, "It's at the jeweler's. One of the prongs broke."

Sookie's unpleasant laugh echoed off the foyer walls. "Oh, really."

"Yes." Livia lifted her chin, a silent challenge. If Sookie *knew* otherwise, then she could prove it. If she'd taken the ring from Mark's bathroom, let her pro-duce it right now. "Really."

"Then why did Reese go running out of here in such a fury after reading this?" Sookie pulled a crumpled piece of paper from a hip pocket and shook it at Livia.

Livia snatched it and smoothed the paper on her leg, then read the crudely printed lettering.

Thought you should know that your fiancée is sleeping with your wedding caterer.

A friend.

Some friend, Livia fumed, her mouth going so dry it felt as though her throat was closing.

"Is it true, Livia? Have you been...sampling that sinfully delicious man...instead of his food?"

Fire flared through Livia, a mishmash of anger and shame and fear. Was Sookie the one who'd broken into Mark's house last night? Had she taken Livia's engagement ring? She considered it a moment and wondered what kind of mother would send her own son a note like this. Even if Sookie killed Wendy, she couldn't imagine the woman purposely hurting Reese. But if she were the killer, if she had broken into Mark's and discovered they were lovers, she might have sent Reese a note so she wouldn't have to tell him to his face and risk his blaming the messenger, to spare him the pain of finding out some other way, all without seeming to be the interfering mother.

Livia asked, "Where did Reese go?"

"He didn't say." Sookie gave a haughty toss of her head. "I've never seen him so upset, spoiling for a fight, like he wanted to smash in someone's face. Where do *you* suppose he went?"

Straight to Mark. Livia felt ill.

The hourglass heated against her breastbone. The kind of heat that prophesied danger. Her fear for Mark sent her rushing out the door, only to remember belatedly their intention to leave a window or door unlatched. Damn it. She'd figure it out when she found Mark. As her car tore down the drive, she grabbed her cell phone, dialing his number before recalling the dead battery.

"Damn it!" She tossed the phone to the passenger seat. Why in hell hadn't she bought one of those car chargers?

The slick streets made rushing impossible, made the drive seem hours long, instead of minutes. With every passing mile, the hourglass grew colder until by the time Livia arrived on Mark's street, she felt the chill clear to her bones.

She pulled into the alleyway and parked next to the van, noting Reese's car on the other side. The house was dark. Too dark. Something was wrong. Very wrong. She grabbed a penlight from the glove box. Rain pelted her and wind whistled over the rooftop as she race to the porch. The door moved inward at the first rap of her knuckles. Livia startled back, her heart tripping.

"Mark?" She stepped into the kitchen, tentative, on guard. "Mark?"

The only sound was the low hum of refrigerators and freezer. "Reese?"

Neither man answered.

She shone the light around the kitchen. Someone had left fresh strawberries and an open container of chocolate sauce on the cutting board. "Mark, where are you?"

She strode to the swinging door and into the room with the fireplace and love seats. She played the light around the room. It was empty. A sound brought her up short. She held her breath, listening hard. A moan or groan. Coming from upstairs. *Mark!* She ran to the staircase.

Dim light glowed from the gaping door to Mark's

private suite. The moaning was louder there. She charged up the stairs and into his living room. The air held a soft, sweet fragrance. Vanilla. "Mark?" No answer. "Reese?"

Another moan—or groan—cut the quiet and she realized what she was hearing were the sounds of lovemaking. She stood stock-still, stunned. Was Mark making love to another woman?

"Oh, Mark." The feminine voice echoed from his bedroom.

Livia's own voice.

Shock riveted her feet to the floor as realization burned through her belly. Whoever had broken in last night had recorded her and Mark making love. She wrestled aside the total sense of violation and forced herself to move to the doorway. Two dozen lighted candles had been spread throughout the room, each giving off a blast of vanilla scent.

A tray on the bed held strawberries, a half-empty bottle of cider, and a bowl with only a film of chocolate sauce remaining in it, as though the chocolate had been consumed in lovemaking, as she and Mark had consumed it last night.

She moved into the room, drawn by the grotesqueness of the scene that last night had been beautiful beyond words but was now just plain eerie. Someone had gone to a lot of trouble. Why? Shivers raced across her skin and a crawly sensation swept her stomach.

"Mark, are you here?"

The hourglass felt like a chip of dry ice against her chest.

With shaking fingers, she found the light switch and flipped it on. Her eyes took a second to adjust, but when they did, she froze. A man's body sprawled face-down on the floor in a pool of dark liquid that seemed to be a gruesome mix of fresh blood and spilled chocolate. A scream ripped up her throat but she clamped her hand over her mouth before it escaped, her gaze locking on the chrome-handled knife with an embossed cupid sticking out of his back. The missing knife.

"Oh, God, Reese."

Was he dead?

Livia dropped to her knees to check for a pulse. As she felt the veins in his neck, she realized his eyes were open, staring, lifeless. Bile climbed in her throat. As she stumbled up and back, she spied her stolen engagement ring in the palm of his outstretched hand.

She fled to the bathroom and gave her dinner to the toilet. When her stomach was empty, she flung open the bathroom window and sucked in the fresh rain-filled air. In the background the tape of her and Mark making love played on, but in the distance, she caught the wail of an approaching siren.

Chapter Eighteen

ALIBI PIZZA PIE

Plenty of Crust
Sauce and Cheese
Whine for All
Stardust Topping

Mark drove through the dark wet streets like a madman, his heart pounding to the beat of the wind against the pickup, to the damned annoying *bump-bump* of the rap music issuing from every stupid speaker. Though he knew everyone, including Livia and Josh, would have left the park the moment the storm burst, he went there first.

Illogical as he knew it was, he felt shivers as he stared at the deserted parking lot. He tried to stay calm, to reason out the motive behind the note and how it fit with the facts he'd gleaned in the Rayburn house. Jay-Ray drove the dark sedan. The money trail led straight to him. He'd handled Wendy's inheritance, was handling what was left of it for Josh. But he, Mark, had followed Jay-Ray home. Had seen the man in the garage and heard him in the house.

There was no way he could have left the note in the pickup.

So, who *had* left the note? The killer, or someone else? He saw the words again in his head. Whoever had written it knew Livia and he were lovers. That might mean the killer and his intruder were not one and the same. So…either two different factions were at work here, or Jay-Ray had an accomplice.

Did one of them have Livia and Josh?

He chided himself not to jump to that conclusion. Not without more proof than a note he suspected was meant to terrify him. But it did terrify him.

He'd prayed all the way across the plateau, all the way down the hill, all the way to the park that the car would still be there, that Livia and Josh would still be there. Even pictured them sitting inside, talking, laughing. Dry. Safe. Oh, God, he shouldn't have left them alone. Pain radiated through his chest and he couldn't suck in a breath.

Take me, God, please, but spare Josh and Livia. I'm not worth much in the scheme of things, but they're both loving and kindhearted, and the world needs more people like that.

He pulled out of the park and back onto the main road, across the I-90 overpass and toward the main section of town. Why didn't she call? He dialed her number for the twentieth time. Got her voice mail again and cursed, choking on his frustration.

He'd already left several messages.

He drove to Jane's Gym, slowly circled the parking area, scanned every slot, every vehicle. Livia's compact wasn't among them. He went next to the Bread and Brew and repeated the parking lot examination, hope dying with every passing second.

He dialed her parents. They hadn't seen her since morning.

He realized with a sinking stomach that he was likely the last one to have seen Josh and her. Why had he left them alone?

All he could think to do was to go home and wait for her to contact him or to show up.

A block from the house he spied her car careering past in the opposite direction. She drove as if chased by demons. He pulled an illegal U-turn, gunned the pickup and caught up to her. Knowing she wouldn't recognize the truck, he honked. Her compact increased speed. He flashed his lights, high beam, low beam. She went faster still.

Finally he pulled into the other lane alongside her and lowered the passenger window so she could see him. "Livia!"

She jolted and glanced his way, eyes full of terror. He saw recognition dawn on her face, followed by relief and something he didn't understand. They both slowed as she lowered her own window and against the driving rain, shouted, "Meet me at the Bread and Brew."

Raising the window, he fell in behind her, following her, putting on notice whoever might have been after her that she was no longer alone, vulnerable.

She skirted the building and parked in the rear of her sister's shop, out of sight of anyone traveling the main street. She scrambled into the pickup cab before he could shift into park and leapt into his arms. "Oh, thank God, Mark. I was so afraid you'd go home before I could find you and stop you."

He held her close, savoring the feel of her, kissing her, never so glad to see someone in his whole life. It took several seconds before he registered that she was shivering hard. He pulled back and peered into her face. "Where is Josh?"

"Home." Her voice trembled. "Safe. Probably in bed by now."

"Thank God. I got this note and I've spent the last hour or more chasing my tail looking for you." He handed her the note. "Why aren't you answering your cell phone?"

"Battery ran down." She read the missive, then touched his face. Even her hand was tremorous. "I'm sorry you were frightened, but you have more to fear than a liar's note."

"What's happened?"

She swallowed as though a rag had lodged in her throat. "Reese is dead…in your bedroom…with one of your knives in his back…and my engagement ring in his hand."

"Dear God, no. No! No!" He searched her face. "Why? How?"

"Reese also received one of these nasty notes, only his told him about us. He rushed to your house to confront you…or us. Oh, Mark, it was awful. A tape recorder was playing. It was of us…making love. Candles. Cider and strawberries and chocolate everywhere, all over Reese's… Reese."

Mark hugged her close again, held her, tried to reassure her, but how could he when his own insides were slipping and sliding like mud in an earthquake? Someone was framing him…again. He'd rather be shot, rather be dead than arrested again for yet another crime he hadn't committed. It was his worst nightmare coming true.

But he had the means to stop it…*if they acted*

quickly. "We can't let the police catch us before we find Wendy's murderer."

"I passed police cars heading to your house as I drove away. They're likely already looking for us or will be soon. How are we going to find Wendy's killer and prove he or she also murdered Reese? We don't have time." She pulled the hourglass from beneath her sweater and showed him that the stardust had fallen to the "1" mark. Tears shone in her aqua eyes. "Not only don't we have time, we don't have a clue where to start looking."

"Ah, but we do, Livia. The money trail led to Jay-Ray." He told her about spotting someone spying on Josh and her, about following the dark sedan from the park and discovering Jay Rayburn had been at the wheel. Then he filled her in on the conversation he'd overheard between Reese and his uncle. "Reese intended to look into Josh's portfolio *and* to start handling it himself. Jay-Ray was livid."

"I can't believe it. Jay gambled away Wendy's and Josh's money? Then killed Wendy and Reese to cover it up." She shuddered. "We have to get into his computer right now, before he has a chance to alter those records."

Even with the time only granules from being gone, she felt a new hope swelling in her chest as they drove the short distance to Rayburn Grocers. But the second they pulled into the parking area, the hope fell flat. "We're too late!" she cried. "Look!"

The dark sedan was parked near the front entrance.

"Wait here," Mark ordered, getting out of the pickup. "I'll confront him."

"No." She hurried to catch up. "We're in this together...until the end. Remember?"

Oblivious to the pouring rain, he kissed her, holding her face in his hands for a long tender moment, memorizing every precious curve. "I'll remember you always. Don't forget that, Livia, no matter what happens in there."

"I won't. Don't you forget, either, that I love you."

He kissed her again.

She said, "We'd better hurry. The hourglass is getting warm. Time is fleeing."

The front door was unlocked and they proceeded cautiously inside. The outer office was quiet, dark, except for the night-light Ali usually left on. They crept toward the hallway, Mark going first as though to protect her, as though he were a shield, a bulletproof vest.

She loved him for it, but feared his foolishness might cost him his life and she wasn't about to let him die, not if she could keep them both alive.

A light shone from Jay-Ray's office. They heard the clack of computer keys. "He's there," she whispered. "Already changing the files."

A woman's voice startled them. "What do you mean, what am I doing? Saving your ass…again."

"I'm perfectly capable of handling my own business," Jay-Ray replied, his voice laced with ire.

They heard a sarcastic feminine huff. "Like hell. You promised you were going to stop this."

"And I meant to. I want to. But something comes over me and I just know I'm going to win. I can't help myself. It's a sickness."

"It's a crime."

"I'm only borrowing the money." Jay-Ray sounded indignant now. "I always replace it."

"No, you don't. You've been losing heavily for

months. You can't replace what you don't have. And now Livia has started asking—''

"Reese is the only one we need to worry about. Livia is all but out of his life. She won't be a problem. Apparently she's set her sights elsewhere. As long as you doctor those files before Reese sees them..."

"Reese won't be seeing Josh's portfolio, Jay." Mark stepped into the office. "He's lying dead on my bedroom floor."

Jay-Ray sat on one corner of his desk and Ali was seated at the computer, hands on the keyboard. Both startled up, gaping at him. Jay said, "Who the hell—"

"Ah, Jay," Ali said. "Let me introduce you to your nephew's fiancée's lover, the wedding caterer, Mark Everett. Or I should say, Ethan Marshall."

"Are you daft?" Jay scowled at Ali. "Ethan Marshall is in prison."

"No," she corrected. "The state found a discrepancy in his case. Some fourth amendment violation and set him free."

Jay-Ray went pure white, then red. He began sputtering, "What...? How...? Why didn't I know about this?"

"We were in Chicago at the playoffs. The story got lost in the coverage of the governor's sexual misconduct case. Ethan Marshall was small potatoes by comparison."

"*You* knew about it. Why didn't you tell me?"

"She seems to protect you from a lot of things, don't you, Ali." Livia moved into the room, glaring down at the buxom brunette.

Jay-Ray was still trying to connect his mental picture of Ethan to Mark. "But you look so different..."

"Prison is hell, Jay-Ray." Mark smirked at him. "But then, you'll be finding that out for yourself soon enough."

Jay's slow gaze crept to Livia. "Is Reese really dead?"

Before she could answer, Ali said, "If he is, it's this man's fault. He's been sleeping with *her*...and Reese found out and went to confront him and now he's dead...just like Wendy, with Ethan's knife in his back."

Livia caught hold of the hourglass, pulling its heat away from her skin. "How did *you* know about the knife, Ali?"

Ali chewed her pinkie finger, giving them her most innocent gaze. "The caterer said so."

"No." Mark shook his head. "I didn't."

"I guess then...I just assumed...since that was the way you killed Wendy."

Mark kept shaking his head at her. "*We* all know I didn't kill Wendy. I didn't have any reason to kill her. I wasn't ripping off her inheritance. *She* was investing it in *our* restaurant. What I can't figure out is why you'd put yourself at such risk for Jay-Ray."

"Someone has to protect him from himself." Ali's chin lifted with pride. "I love him. And he loves me. He's going to marry me."

"If he was going to marry you," Livia said, "why hasn't he in the three years since you murdered Wendy for him?"

"You murdered Wendy?" Jay-Ray looked stunned.

"Of course not," Ali protested. She pointed an accusing finger at Mark. *"He did!"*

"Think about it, Jay," Mark argued. "Why was

Wendy killed in your office? She'd been to see you about her money, hadn't she?"

"Yes. She wanted everything converted to cash on her birthday. Everything. *She* was going to start handling her own money. She wouldn't listen to reason, wouldn't reconsider. But I couldn't let her discover there were funds missing."

"So, *you* killed her," Livia said.

"God, no. I set up a meeting with the banker, to mortgage the warehouse. But they wouldn't lend me the money without Phillip's signature."

"And Phillip wasn't so sick that he didn't know you were trying to mortgage the business to pay off gambling debts." Mark was getting in Jay-Ray's face, making Jay uncomfortable, giving him a taste of what to expect in prison. "So, you went crying to Ali."

"She said she could fix it for me. I promised to marry her if she did. But, Ethan, er, you murdered Wendy and my problems went away." He snapped his fingers. "Just like that."

Livia snapped her fingers, too. "And just like that you didn't have to marry Ali, did you?"

"No." He grinned.

Ali's face went beet-red.

"And Ali was stuck in a Catch-22." Livia realized, pieces of the puzzle falling together with ease now. "If she told you what she'd done for you to get you off the hook, you'd have had her arrested."

Mark took over, pointing at Jay, backing him into a corner of the room. "But that would have made you an accessory. So, you told yourself she couldn't have done what you feared she had—because you couldn't stop gambling."

"I have a problem, man," Jay-Ray whined. "I can't

help it. It's worse than any drug. But I've bet on a sure thing tonight that will pay off big tomorrow. More than enough to repay the funds I borrowed from Josh's accounts.''

''You've known all along that he was ripping off my children and didn't tell me?'' Sookie stood in the doorway, glaring at Ali. She'd entered so quietly her presence was startling. Her face was as pale as death. She looked like a candle whose flame had been doused, and Livia knew in her heart that she had learned of Reese's murder. But how long had she been there; what had she heard?

Sookie continued to glare at Ali. ''He depleted Wendy's inheritance and you helped him cover it up?''

''Jay-Ray is a star. A celebrity.'' Ali gave a toss of her dark hair. ''He's worth ten of the rest of you. What do you care where he got the money as long as it wasn't from you?''

''Oh, I do care about someone stealing money from my daughter and my grandson.''

''Your *step*daughter, the wicked witch of the north, south, east and west.'' Ali let loose a sarcastic laugh. ''Don't go all maternal on us, Sookie.''

''You're right. There was no love lost between Wendy and me.'' Sookie moved closer to Ali. ''But I admired the way she stood up to her father, proving to him that women were more than arm candy and broodmares. Did she find out you'd robbed her, Jay? Is that why she died in your office?''

''She was going to call the police,'' Ali said, easing open the top desk drawer and reaching inside.

Alarm shot through Livia and she looked for something to toss at Ali.

Ali was looking at Sookie. "She threatened to have Jay arrested."

Sookie glanced at her brother-in-law. "*You* murdered Wendy and—" she choked "—my Reese?"

"Of course not." Jay-Ray was as pale as Sookie.

"He hasn't the guts, Sookie," Mark put in, moving back across the office to stand between Livia and the redhead. "It's why he was drummed off the Sonics' roster. He's a wuss."

Livia snatched a thick food catalog from atop a file cabinet. When Ali pulled the gun from the drawer, Livia would fling the catalog like a Frisbee and knock the revolver from her grip. Fear and hope filled Livia as she clutched the catalog to her thundering heart and scooted nearer Ali. She wasn't going to lose Mark and she wasn't going to die. Not at Ali's hand.

"You saw the way her father treated her." Hatred the only thing alive in her eyes, Sookie stalked toward Jay, who still hunched against the window. "How could you steal from her the one thing she needed, rob her of her one triumph?"

Jay had no answer. He cringed back from the insult, would have run for the door, Livia suspected, had the way not been barred by all of them. Ali pulled her hand smoothly from the drawer. Livia spied something silver in her grip and inched closer.

"Who killed her?" Sookie demanded, pivoting. "If not Jay, then who? Which one of you killed my daughter?"

Only then did Livia realize Ali gripped a knife from Mark's kitchen. But Sookie held a small pistol in her palm. She aimed it at the brunette. "You, Ali?"

She swung the barrel toward Livia. "You?"

Ali brought the knife into view.

Mark stepped between Sookie and Livia, and Sookie leveled the gun at him. "Or the man who killed my son? You…Ethan."

"No." Livia had to choose between stopping Ali from throwing the knife and Sookie from shooting Mark.

Sookie pulled back the hammer.

"No! Mark is innocent! Ali killed Reese and Wendy!" Livia dropped the album and leapt at Mark, shoving him out of the way.

The gun blast resounded in her ears at the exact moment she felt the bullet tear through her flesh. She heard someone scream and realized it was Sookie.

Chaos seemed to explode in the room.

Livia felt a burning pain, felt the world going black, felt Mark catch her as she slipped to the floor. The hourglass had gone deadly cold again and she didn't need to see it to know that the stardust had drained to zero.

"I love you, Mark. Be strong for Josh."

She should have known she couldn't make bargains with Heaven. Couldn't cheat Fate. Her only consolation was that Mark would have his son again, and Josh would have his daddy. For that she gladly paid this ultimate price.

The last thing she heard was Mark calling her name. The last thing she saw was his golden eyes so like the light for which her soul headed.

Chapter Nineteen

ANGELS' FOOD

Bright Light
Haloes and Wings
Processing
Heavenly Sentence

Mark's eyes faded in the blare of the bright light pulling Livia upward, but nothing could strip her of his memory or the way he'd made her feel. That was seared so deeply into her spirit it would be with her through eternity.

As before, she seemed to be walking without feeling solid substance—floor or pavement or ground—beneath her feet. She noticed no noise or sound, until a sudden dull roar, like static, stole into the quietude.

She sensed she was not alone, that others, unseen, walked with her, beside her, ahead of her, behind her. She felt unseen hands bump against her like offers of sympathy.

She deserved no sympathy.

No forgiveness.

She'd been callous and full of herself the last time

she'd faced the Processor, outraged that she'd ended up dead on the eve of her marriage to a man she'd chosen for all the wrong reasons. *Then* she'd thought she understood the importance of life: money, status, and staying forever thin. *Then* she'd figured it was more important for her to live than some hapless chef she'd never met.

Now she knew nothing was more important than to love and be loved in return. Maybe Heaven would have granted Mark and her a long life together *if* she had also followed the physician's credo: First, Do No Harm.

But she hadn't.

She'd been given a chance to change things so that she could keep herself from getting shot and dying. *She'd changed things, all right.* She'd fallen in love with her caterer, which had led to her fiancé's murder. She'd wished Reese no harm. Certainly hadn't wanted him to die. But because of her actions, he had. She would never forgive herself for that. Heaven would certainly never forgive such a sin.

In fact, she wouldn't be surprised to discover she was on her way to Hell this time around.

She didn't seem to be descending, however, but rising; floating, weightless and as airy as fluff on the wind, sailing upward toward a destination she could not see.

She was not frightened this time, nor hesitant. She'd known what would happen if she took another bullet meant for Mark. She'd taken it willingly. Would take any consequence due her. The airy feeling left and she now seemed to be gliding along as though on a motorized walkway.

Soon, the light began to dim.

Ahead, she made out shapes. Outlines. Gauzy, but recognizable, slowly emerging as if from a fog of light. People. Three women and two men. Beyond them, the image clearer than the others, stood a tall figure in a hooded robe of pure white silk, the edges trimmed in gold. The Processor. Behind him stood the massive, solid-gold gate, its filigree scrolls as sparkly as a diamond tiara.

She hadn't been sent to Hell.

Livia felt humbled. This was better than she deserved.

A sense of peace hung in the air so palpable she could taste it, smell it, touch it, but she felt no peace knowing that Reese had traveled this same path hours before her, been processed through that mesmerizing gate and into Heaven before his time...because of her actions. What she felt was an awful guilt. Loneliness. Inevitability.

And then it was her turn.

The Processor lifted his head and beneath the pristine hood she saw her grandfather Poppy's face. Saw the eyes widen in dismay and braced herself.

"Oh, no," the Processor said, tsking in his best Poppy voice. "Not you again. And early, too."

"I know." Only then did Livia realize the golden hourglass no longer hung from her neck. "I changed all the wrong things, I guess."

"Well, you know what this means." He seemed as sadly resigned as she felt.

"Yes. But maybe I don't belong here at all."

"What?"

"Maybe I belong...you know..." She pointed toward her feet. "Down there."

"Down?" His eyes widened. "In Hell? Why would you say that?"

"Why would I say that? Don't you know I've caused my fiancé's death? I'm sure you processed him through earlier." She pointed to the golden gate this time. "Reese Rayburn?"

"You say you murdered him?" He consulted his computer.

"No, but—"

"His name is not in my files." Silk swished as he shook his head at her. "If he was murdered, he didn't come here."

She considered that a minute, deciding for all his faults, Reese wasn't a bad man, couldn't have done anything so awful he'd have gone to Hell. There had to be another explanation. She pointed at the computer. "Are you sure you're spelling his name correctly? *R-e-e-s-e R-a-y-b-u-r-n?*"

He worked the keyboard again. "Oh, he is here."

Even though she expected this, her heart sank. "Before his time...like me."

"Oh, no." The Processor peered at her with Poppy's kind eyes. "He's just a couple of weeks early, but not before his time. He died as he was supposed to have. Stabbed with a knife, right?"

"Yes. Stabbed." *Reese was supposed to have died before their wedding?* Livia struggled to make sense of this. "I guess I wasn't getting married on February twenty-eighth no matter what I did, even if I'd lived, even if I hadn't fallen in love with another man?"

"I remember you like to ask questions," the Processor said. "But you've forgotten that I don't have the answers. All I do is process souls into Heaven."

Livia was trying to process the fact that Reese had

been slated to die. As she thought about it, though, she realized it made sense. Was even inevitable. He'd sealed his own fate the moment Ali discovered he'd decided to check into Jay-Ray's handling of Josh's money.

I've been giving myself too much credit, too much power, as though I controlled life and death. She blushed, chagrined. Talk about someone needing an ego check. "I guess you'd better process me."

"Yes. My hands are tied. We must proceed."

He seemed so sad, she felt the need to reassure him. "It's okay. It's not your fault. I could have avoided the bullet, but I did what I did on purpose and I'd do it all over again, even if you gave me another chance to change the outcome. In other words, I'm ready and willing to go in Mark Everett's place."

"My, but you are a changed woman, aren't you?"

More than she'd ever thought possible.

His hands sped across the keyboard. "There, that's it. Step over to the gate and as soon as it swings inward, you'll see loved ones who've gone before waiting for you.

Livia started to walk past the Processor.

"Livia Kingston!" A golden voice rang down from above like the toll of a bell and stopped her in her tracks.

"Yes?" she whispered, her mouth dry. *Here it comes, she thought, I'm going straight to Hell for trying to alter God's divine plans, for saving Mark, for trying to keep us both alive when I'd been told specifically that one of us had to die.*

But she'd promised herself she would take her punishment, and she would—without allowing them to see the fear that threatened to turn her to jelly. With every ounce of will she could muster, she squared her shoulders and raised her chin.

"Yes," she said, loud and clear. "I am Livia Kingston."

"Livia Kingston—by giving up your life for the sake of another, you have shown great courage and selflessness." The imperial voice tolled. "Such deeds do not go unrewarded."

This didn't sound like a ticket to the underworld. This sounded like good news. Rewarded. How did they reward someone in Heaven?

With a halo?

Wings?

"Livia Kingston!" the voice boomed. "You have learned the lesson set before you and redeemed yourself."

Redeemed myself? "I did?"

"Yes, and in doing so, you have earned the right to live."

What? She gave her head a shake. *Did your hearing leave when you died?* It must. He couldn't have said what she thought He had.

She frowned, asking, "The right to *live?* As in *alive? Breathing? Heart beating? Pulse pounding? Alive?*"

"There she goes again." The Processor sighed. "Questioning everything, repeating everything."

"What about Mark? If I get my life back will he lose his? Because you should know that I don't want to be alive without him. I don't want his son to lose him."

"No. You have saved Mark Everett as well as yourself."

"Oh, thank you. Thank you."

"Livia Kingston," the golden voice bellowed, "I sentence you to life and love!"

With that came a clap as loud as thunder, followed by a blinding flash of light. She squeezed her eyes shut and moaned. The next instant she became aware of noise all around her, rain, voices and the static of a police scanner. Strobe lights seemed to blink behind her eyelids.

Mark's voice cut through it all, reaching out to her. "Livia, can you hear me?"

She pried open her eyes and stared into that golden gaze of his, and awareness splashed through her. He was holding her hand, running beside her as two EMTs wheeled the stretcher she was strapped to toward a waiting ambulance.

She breathed in the wet night air, felt an awful pain in her side and a wondrous joy that she was alive to feel it. "Yes, darling, oh, yes, I hear you. I'm going to live."

He looked worried, as though he didn't believe her. "I can't go in the ambulance with you, but I'll follow it to the hospital."

"Okay. And stop worrying, I'm going to be fine. We're going to be together this Valentine's Day and every other one to come."

Mark stepped back and they lifted Livia into the ambulance. As he started toward Candee's pickup, she saw two uniformed police officers and a man in a suit approach him. The plainclothes officer flashed his detective's badge. "Mark Everett?"

"Yes." Mark went rigid.

"You're under arrest for the murder of Reese Rayburn.'' The detective slapped handcuffs on him, then barked to the other officers, "Read him his rights and don't mess up. He's not getting off on a technicality this time.''

Epilogue

WEDDING TOAST

Something Old
Something New
Something Bubbly
Nothing Blue

July

Celebratory voices echoed off the walls of the Old Grange Hall, underscored by the swinging beat of the six piece dance band. This was not the formal, upscale wedding reception Livia had expected when she'd planned on marrying a Rayburn. This was the Kingston clan in all its generations, its full glory, loud, laughing, raucous, the noise level deafening.

She had never appreciated being part of it as she did this day.

She gripped Mark's hand and leaned in to whisper above the din, "Get used to it. You haven't married just me, but the whole family."

"Good." Mark turned his joy-filled gaze on her, making her feel downright sinful in her virgin-white satin and lace, as though she wore the skimpiest, most man-luring scrap of red-hot lingerie.

She'd known this plain-Jane off-the-shoulder dress was "the" gown the moment she'd tried it on, the moment she'd seen that sensuous gleam of approval in Mark's eyes. But after being shot, she'd feared she wouldn't be able to wear anything that clung to her as this did, feared the scar would show. The bullet wound had left a puckered divot at her waist, front and back, a permanent reminder of how close she'd come to losing all that was precious to her in this life.

As though he read her mind, Mark said, "You've gotten us with all of our warts, too."

He gazed toward his son, who played with two of her nephews, boys being boys, starting a mini food fight. The joy in his eyes dimmed slightly as Josh forgot the play and glanced their way. In his child's tuxedo, he appeared to be a happy, normal little boy, but he'd been going through a clingy stage since being reunited with his daddy, and even today, especially today, though he was better, he seemed to need reassurance that they weren't going to disappear on him.

On the advice of their family therapist, they'd decided to postpone their honeymoon for a couple of weeks, to stop Josh from associating big events with abandonment. He'd had enough upheaval in his young life.

"Aren't you two hungry?" Charlie Kingston, Livia's dad, set his overflowing plate on their table. "You should see the spread. Bridget and Candee done you proud."

"Wait until you taste the cake, Dad." Livia had Mark to thank for helping her conquer her fear of sweets. Especially cake. "Bridget outdid herself."

He leaned closer and lowered his voice, glanced toward the buffet table, then back at Livia and Mark. "Between you two and me, I suspect I'm gonna be throwing another one of these shindigs in another few months. Every time Bridget and your partner glance at each other, they wind up all moony-eyed."

Livia and Mark laughed. It was true. Somewhere along the way while sharing banquet preparations for the reception, Candee and Bridget had begun paying as much attention to each other as to the food, and now her sister had set her sights on Mark's partner. The grand thing was, the feelings seemed mutual.

"It's been a wild five months," Mark said, pulling her chair out so they could hit the buffet line.

Livia smiled as she passed relatives and friends, accepted kisses and hugs and more congratulations. She couldn't believe all that had happened since Mark had been arrested and she'd been hurried off to the hospital and into surgery. She'd been fortunate in that the bullet had missed every vital organ and major artery.

Mark had been less fortunate. The district attorney had claimed to have an open-and-shut case against him and had been dead-set on the death penalty. But he'd wanted a solid case without mistakes. To that end, he'd listened to Livia and Sookie and eventually to Mark. He'd checked into Jay-Ray's misappropriation of funds, his criminal handling of both Josh's and Wendy's monies, found proof of embezzlement, and charged him as an accessory to two homicides.

Jay-Ray had offered to give up Ali and his lawyers plea-bargained him to a lighter sentence in exchange for that evidence. It helped that the police had also found her fingerprint on the audio tape of Livia and Mark making love, which Ali had used to lure Reese to Mark's bedroom, to his death. The idea of all those detectives and lawyers listening to that private tape made Livia blush, but it was a small price to pay for Mark's freedom, his complete exoneration.

Sookie had had a nervous breakdown after shooting Livia and was still undergoing counseling.

Though none of Josh's gambled money could be recovered, Reese had left him his share of Rayburn Roost and Rayburn Grocers Inc. The business had been sold, Josh's half put into a trust fund no one could touch without going through several lawyers and bank officials.

Her father called, "A toast to the happy couple."

A hush fell over the hall and everyone lifted their glasses. Love poured from their faces and into Livia's heart.

She squeezed Mark's hand, hugged Josh between them, and listened as first her father, then her uncles began giving a round of toasts, an old family tradition that would take a long while to get through.

The smile seemed to bloom from somewhere inside her, spreading to her lips, her eyes, and radiating out to all who looked on her. There was no rush, no hourglass counting down the minutes of her life. All the time in the world stretched before her. All the time that Heaven allowed.

Livia wasn't going to miss a second of it.

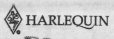

HARLEQUIN

INTRIGUE

COMING NEXT MONTH

#697 HER HIDDEN TRUTH by Debra Webb
The Specialists

When CIA agent Katrina Moore's memory implant malfunctioned while she was under deep cover, her only hope for rescue lay with Vince Ferrelli. Only, Kat and Vince shared a tumultuous past, which threatened to sabotage their mission. Could Vince save Kat—and restore her memories—before it was too late?

#698 HEIR TO SECRET MEMORIES by Mallory Kane
Top Secret Babies

After he was brutally attacked and left for dead, Jay Wellcome lost all of his memories. His only recollection: the image of a nameless beauty. And though Jay never anticipated they'd come face-to-face, when Paige Reynolds claimed she needed him—honor demanded he offer his protection. Paige's daughter had been kidnapped and nothing would stop him from tracking a killer—especially when he learned her child was also his....

#699 THE ROOKIE by Julie Miller
The Taylor Clan

For the youngest member of the Taylor clan, Josh Taylor, an undercover assignment to smoke out drug dealers on a university campus could promote him to detective. Only, Josh never anticipated his overwhelming feelings for his pregnant professor Rachel Livesay. And when the single mother-to-be's life was threatened by a stalker named "Daddy," Josh's protective instincts took over. But would Rachel accept his protection...and his love?

#700 CONFESSIONS OF THE HEART by Amanda Stevens

Fully recovered from her heart transplant surgery, Anna Sebastian was determined to start a new life. But someone was determined to thwart her plans.... With her life in jeopardy, tough-as-nails cop Ben Porter was the only man she could trust. And now in a race against time, could Ben and Anna uncover the source of the danger before she lost her second chance?

Visit us at www.eHarlequin.com

HARLEQUIN®
INTRIGUE®

Opens the case files on:

TOP SECRET BABIES

Unwrap the mystery!

January 2003
THE SECRET SHE KEEPS
BY CASSIE MILES

February 2003
HEIR TO
SECRET MEMORIES
BY MALLORY KANE

March 2003
CLAIMING HIS FAMILY
BY ANN VOSS PETERSON

Follow the clues to your favorite retail outlet!

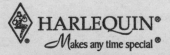

HARLEQUIN®
Makes any time special ®

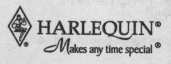

HARLEQUIN®
INTRIGUE®

***Elevates breathtaking romantic suspense
to a whole new level!***

When all else fails, the most highly trained, covert
agents are called in to "recover" the mission.
This elite group is known as

THE SPECIALISTS

Nothing is too dangerous for them…
except falling in love.

DEBRA WEBB

does it again with an explosive new trilogy for Harlequin
Intrigue. You'll recognize some of the names from her
popular COLBY AGENCY series, but hang on to your
hats this time out. Because THE SPECIALISTS are more
dangerous, more daring…and more deadly than any agents
you've ever seen!

UNDERCOVER WIFE
January

HER HIDDEN TRUTH
February

GUARDIAN OF THE NIGHT
March

Look for them wherever Harlequin books are sold!

HARLEQUIN®
Makes any time special ®

For more on Harlequin Intrigue® books, visit www.tryintrigue.com   HISPEC